Berkley Sensation titles by Gena Showalter

MAGIC AT MIDNIGHT

Anthologies

MYSTERIA

(with P. C. Cast, MaryJanice Davidson, and Susan Grant)

MYSTERIA LANE

(with P. C. Cast, MaryJanice Davidson, and Susan Grant)

MYSTERIA NIGHTS

(with P. C. Cast, MaryJanice Davidson, and Susan Grant)

Magic at Midnight

GENA SHOWALTER

BERKLEY SENSATION, NEW YORK

THE BERKLEY PUBLISHING GROUP
Published by the Penguin Group
Penguin Group (USA) Inc.
375 Hudson Street, New York, New York 10014, USA
Penguin Group (Canada), 90 Eglinton Avenue East, Suite 700, Toronto, Ontario M4P 2Y3, Canada (a division of Pearson Penguin Canada Inc.) • Penguin Books Ltd., 80 Strand, London WC2R 0RL, England • Penguin Ireland, 25 St. Stephen's Green, Dublin 2, Ireland (a division of Penguin Books Ltd.) • Penguin Group (Australia), 707 Collins Street, Melbourne, Victoria 3008, Australia (a division of Pearson Australia Group Pty. Ltd.) • Penguin Books India Pvt. Ltd., 11 Community Centre, Panchsheel Park, New Delhi—110 017, India • Penguin Group (NZ), 67 Apollo Drive, Rosedale, Auckland 0632, New Zealand (a division of Pearson New Zealand Ltd.) • Penguin Books (South Africa), Rosebank Office Park, 181 Jan Smuts Avenue, Parktown North 2193, South Africa • Penguin China, B7 Jiaming Center, 27 East Third Ring Road North, Chaoyang District, Beijing 100020, China

Penguin Books Ltd., Registered Offices: 80 Strand, London WC2R 0RL, England

MAGIC AT MIDNIGHT

Cover images by Shutterstock. Cover design by Jason Gill.
Interior text design by Kristen del Rosario.

PUBLISHING HISTORY
"The Witches of Mysteria and the Dead Who Love Them" previously published in *Mysteria* / July 2006
"A Tawdry Affair" previously published in *Mysteria Lane* / October 2008
"The Witches of Mysteria and the Dead Who Love Them" and "A Tawdry Affair"
previously published in *Mysteria Nights* / July 2011
Berkley Sensation trade paperback edition / February 2013

Berkley Sensation trade paperback edition ISBN: 978-0-425-26538-3

An application to register this book for cataloging has been submitted to the Library of Congress.

PRINTED IN THE UNITED STATES OF AMERICA

10 9 8 7 6 5 4 3 2 1

CONTENTS

INTRODUCTION

Once upon a time in a land closer than anyone might be comfortable with, a demon high lord was sent to destroy a small, starving (and, let's face it, weird) band of settlers who were fleeing the last town they'd tried to settle in (a place eventually known as Kansas City, Missouri, the Show Me State, which did indeed show them tar and feathers and the road west). The group was composed of magical misfits and outcasts: a bloodaphobic vampire, a black-magic witch and her white-magic husband, a pack of amorous (translation: hump-happy) werewolves, and a man named John, who had gotten confused and joined the wrong wagon train. When the demon spied this ragged, rejected bunch, he (for a reason known only to himself but which had to do with uncontrollable random acts of kindness) decided not just to spare them but to create a magical haven for them.

And so, nestled in a beautiful valley in the Rocky Mountains, the town of Mysteria was founded. Over the years, it became a refuge for creatures of the night and those unwanted by traditional society. No one—or thing—was turned away. Magic thrived, aphrodisiacs laced the pollen, and fairy tales came true.

The first settlers eventually died (those that weren't already dead or undead, that is), but they left pieces of themselves behind. The vampire invented a powerful blood-appetite suppressant for any other vampires with a fear of blood. The witch and the warlock created a wishing well—a wishing well that swirled and churned with both white and black magic, a dangerous combination. The hump-happy werewolves left the essence of perpetual springtime and love (translation: they peed all around the boundary of the city, so that everyone—or thing—that entered or left Mysteria was, well, marked). John, the only nonmagical being in the group, left his confused but mundane genes, founding a family that would ultimately spawn more humans of nonmagical abilities who remained in Mysteria because finding their way out was just too much like geometry.

Each of the settlers thought, as their spirits floated to the heavens—all right, some of them went straight to hell, the naughty sinners—that their best contribution to the fantastical town of Mysteria was a happily-ever-after for their descendants. If only they could have known the events that would one day unfold . . .

The Witches of Mysteria and the Dead Who Love Them

To those of us who probably should live in Mysteria:
P. C. Cast, Susan Grant, and MaryJanice Davidson.
And to Christine Zika for a wonderful experience.

· One ·

"MEN suck," Genevieve Tawdry muttered, "and not in a good way."

She was tired, so very tired, of Hunter Knight's hot and cold treatment of her. He was making her crazy, laughing with her flirtatiously one moment (translation: stringing her along without giving her any actual benefits, the bastard), then dropping her altogether the next moment, then laughing flirtatiously with her again.

She wasn't going to tolerate it anymore.

Unfortunately, lovesick witch that she was, Genevieve didn't have the strength to shove him from her life—which meant she would have to up her game. But how? Truly, she'd tried everything. Spells and incantations. "Accidental" meetings where she happened to be braless. "Accidentally" ramming her car into the back end of his Ford Explorer. Or the latest, an incident that happened only last night, "accidentally" tripping and falling into his lap at a mutual friend's wedding.

Nothing worked.

Last night had been a "cold" night. Hunter had taken one look at her in her brand-new white silk dress (no, she hadn't been the bride and yes, the bride had been pissed that she'd dared to wear the "sacred" color) and he hadn't been able to get away from her fast enough. She sighed.

What would it take to make herself irresistible to him? To hold his attention for as long as she desired it? To at last put an end to the heart-pounding tension that always sparked between them when they were together? Whatever was needed, she'd do it. Anything. Everything.

"I'm seriously a stalker." Frowning, she tapped her fingers against the desk surface.

Moonlight spilled through the window in front of her, mingling with the soft glow of lamplight, illuminating the unread book in front of her. Incense burned beside her, the scent of jasmine curling sweetly and fragrancing the air.

She sat in the office of the three-bedroom home, aka den of iniquity, she shared with her two sisters, hunched over the desk, dark strands of hair falling over her shoulders. Behind her, the TV emitted a *crunch, crunch* sound, as if someone on-screen was enjoying a tasty snack. A family of squirrels raced around her feet—her oldest sister's newest save-the-world-one-animal-at-a-time "project."

I don't want to be Hunter's stalker. I want to be his lover.

Over the years, he had become the bane of her existence, the mountain she'd tried to climb (naked) but couldn't quite manage to conquer. But damn it. He liked her; she knew he did. Last night, before he'd run away from her, she would have sworn he'd had an erection and had been desperate to get *to* her, not away. Desperate to touch her. Desperate to taste her.

Heat had blazed in his emerald eyes, scorching, white-hot. Enough to blister. He'd reached for her, his fingers caressing her with phantom strokes, before he dropped his arm to his side. He'd licked his lips and taken a step toward her before catching himself and striding away.

Why, why, *why* did he continually do crap like that?

If not for moments like those, she might have given up long ago and forced herself to forget him. Yet, he'd beaten John Foster to a bloody pulp for trying to kiss her. He always walked her home if he saw her in town. And it was *her* he'd called when his father had died, seeking comfort. *Her* he came to when he had a problem at work and needed help finding a solution.

That meant something. Didn't it?

"Maybe you should offer to ride him like a carnival pony," Glory said from behind her. "That always works for me."

Genevieve twisted to face her younger sister. "What are you doing in here?" she gasped out in surprise.

Glory brushed away the cheese dust on her lips. "Uh, spying. Hello. I say sleep with some other man and forget Hunter."

Always the same advice. Genevieve eased slowly to her feet. "How would you like it if I cast a spell, bringing every one of those chips to life and letting them exact their revenge against you?"

Glory's hazel eyes flashed. "You wouldn't dare!"

"Oh, really? Keep talking, then, and by tomorrow morning the entire town will be talking about the Great Doritos Death."

"Is that before or after they talk about Stalkerella and her unwilling victim?"

For several seconds, she and Glory glared at each other. Hunter was a sore spot for Genevieve; food was a sore spot for Glory.

Finally Glory expelled a deep breath, and her features slowly softened. "Evie, when are you going to realize Hunter will never want you the way you want him? He dates everything that moves and even some things that don't. But not you. Never you. He just, well, I didn't want to be the one to tell you this, but he pities you."

"He does not."

"Yes, he does."

"No, he *desires* me."

"That's delusion talking, and something *every* stalker says."

"I'm not stalking him," she said with a stubborn tilt of her chin, even though she herself had thought the very same thing. "I'm seducing him."

Her sister rolled her eyes and popped another chip in her mouth. "That's like saying murdering your neighbor is merely giving them a big send-off."

"Girls, please." Godiva, the oldest sister, strode into the room, her silver-white hair streaming behind her. She wore ripped jeans and a faded blue T-shirt, both of which were streaked with blood, dirt, and dark fur. "I've got an injured wolf in the kitchen and your arguing is upsetting him."

"You brought an injured wolf into the house?" All traces of color abandoned Glory's cheeks. "I can live with the squirrels and the wood mice, but a wolf? No way. They're dangerous killers, Diva. They like to claw witches like us into bite-sized nibblets and feast on the pieces."

"We have nothing to fear from him." Godiva anchored her hands on her hips. "He's too weak to cause us any harm."

"Where is he?" Genevieve asked, trying to push Hunter—and Glory's remarks—to the back of her mind. Her sister didn't understand. How could she? She'd never been in love, never been consumed by the emotion. Never wanted more from a man than temporary satisfaction.

"He's in the kitchen, and I could use your help."

"Of course." Following behind her older sister, Genevieve dragged a protesting Glory down the hall and into the kitchen.

Glory immediately flattened herself against the wall, surrounding herself with faux plant leaves, maintaining a safe distance from the large—very large—animal lying on the black and white tiled floor. As if she could hide with hair as vivid red as hers. Godiva bent over him, dabbing a steaming cloth over the jagged, bleeding claw wounds on his belly. He whimpered up at her, his eyes big and brown and glazed with pain.

Genevieve crouched beside her oldest sister. "What do you need me to do?"

They spent the next several hours murmuring peace spells, applying salve, and stitching the poor wolf's wounds. He drifted in and out of sleep, but through it all he responded to Godiva's every touch, recognizing her voice, her scent, and calming whenever she approached.

"He likes you," Genevieve said.

"I think he recognizes me and feels safe. I've seen him before, in the forest. I was gathering herbs, and he was watching me."

Genevieve wished Hunter responded to her half as much as this wolf responded to her sister. Since the day Hunter had saved her from gracing the dessert menu of a rabid gnome, she'd loved him.

She'd been seventeen years old at the time and he twenty-two, but she'd known she belonged with him. They'd even kissed that day, a delicious, mind-shattering kiss she'd never forgotten. Yes, she'd relived it in her dreams over and over again.

They were meant to be together, damn it. The way he sometimes treated her like a curse of hemorrhoids, no anti-itch cream in sight, had to stop! Did he think she meant to use him as a sexual toy then kick him out of her life? If so, he should love that. Did he think she meant to ruin their friendship? Well, she didn't. She wanted to love him (hard core).

She would never, ever do anything to hurt him. Well . . . she bit her bottom lip. Fine. That wasn't exactly true. Once she'd cast a seduction spell over him, hoping he would become sexually enthralled with the first woman he saw (which would have been her). Instead, she'd made nearly every woman in Mysteria, a town known for its weirdness, fall into instant lust with *him*. Even her sisters had been trapped under the spell. For days the entire female population had followed him everywhere, ripping at his clothes, begging him to make love to them.

"Even if the wolf saw you before," Glory said, the sound of her voice breaking into Genevieve's thoughts, "that's not reason enough for him to respond so favorably to you. He acts like he adores you." She frowned. "Hey, did you give him one of my love potions?"

"Of course not," Godiva said. "I think he senses that I mean him no harm."

At Glory's words, a wonderfully frightening idea danced inside Genevieve's mind, an idea she'd always discarded before—and no, she wasn't going to injure Hunter to gain his attention (although she wouldn't rule that out, the sexy bastard). What if *she* drank a love potion? What if she made herself so irresistible he wouldn't think of turning her away? She'd never dared drink one before; there were simply too many uncertain variables.

For one night in his arms, though, she was now willing to risk it. Risk the deflation of her inhibitions, the danger of enticing the love of a legion of other men. The danger of loving him forever and him only loving her for a single night. Hell, she already loved him and she didn't see an end in sight for the emotion. For Hunter, she'd risk anything. Everything. Except . . .

Genevieve uttered a sigh. Did she really want to win him because of a potion and not because he simply wanted *her*? Yes, she decided in the next instant. The stubborn man needed a push in the right direction, and she was tired of waiting for that to happen naturally. Her patience was frayed beyond repair.

Besides, if she had to watch him flirt and laugh with another woman one more time, just one more time, she'd fly into a rampage worthy of the Desdaine triplets, the town's most notorious troublemakers.

Now that she had a plan, urgency rushed through her. She glanced at the clock above the refrigerator. Ten P.M.

Knight Caps, Hunter's bar, would be open for at least four more hours.

"Will you be okay on your own?" she asked Godiva.

"Hey, she's not alone. *I'm* here," Glory said with a pout.

"Oh, sorry. Will you be okay with Glory standing in the shadows and doing nothing?"

"I'll be fine." Godiva nodded. "Candy Cox should be here any minute. She's going to sit with me." Candy—oops, *Candice*—was the high school English teacher and Godiva's best friend. "My big boy is finally resting peacefully. Why? Are you going out?"

"Yes." She offered no other explanation. Neither of her sisters approved of her obsession with Hunter.

"Where are you going?" Glory asked suspiciously. She inched to the kitchen table, keeping the long length of the hand-carved mahogany between herself and the wolf.

"I'm. Going. Out."

"That's not what I meant and you know it." She paused, then her pretty face scrunched in disgust. "You're going to see *him*, aren't you?"

Genevieve's back went ramrod straight. "So what if I am? You got something to say about it?"

"Nope. Not a word. Except, if you want to make a fool of yourself over him again, go for it. Just know that the town isn't laughing *with* you, they're laughing *at* you."

Her fists clenched at her sides. "You're just begging for a piece of me, Glor."

Awakening, the wolf raised his head, his lips pulling tight over his fangs.

"Don't listen to them," Godiva cooed at him. She smothered her fingers over his thick fur, giving her sisters a pointed glare. "They're showing their stupidity, and it's quite embarrassing."

"We're not embarrassing," Glory said. "You're embarrassing! You treat that mutt better than you treat your beloved sisters."

"With good reason."

As they argued, anticipation and nervousness zinged through Genevieve's veins. Not for the proposed trip into hell, but for the coming night. Now that she'd decided to do it, to love-potion the pants right off of Hunter, she didn't want to waste another minute. "Glory, I'd like to talk with you privately," she said sweetly. She motioned to the living room with a tilt of her chin. "I don't want to fight."

"I don't believe you."

"Okay, stay here then. I'm sure the wolf won't regain full strength soon and be disoriented and afraid. He won't fly into a rampage and—"

Glory jolted backward with a gasp. "Alright. Fine." One tiny step, two, she scooted around the table, around the wolf. "I'll meet you in the living room."

Dissatisfied with such a gradual pace, Genevieve reached out, grabbed her younger sister's hand, and tugged her into the next room. In the center, she whirled. She was almost bubbling over. Tonight might be the night all her dreams came true. . . . Glory's love potions were legendary. Each sister specialized in a different area of magic. While she herself wielded the darkest power, that over vengeance, Godiva's strength was in healing, both spiritual and physical, and Glory's was in love.

"I want to drink one of your love potions. And don't say no."

Glory pursed her lips and crossed her arms over her chest. "How about: hell, no."

"Please."

"Nein. Nay. Non."

She pushed out a frustrated breath. "Why not?"

"Evie," her sister said, her expression softening, "he's not good enough for you. When are you going to realize that? I'm more inclined to turn him into an impotent troll than help you win his affections."

"It's one night, Glor. What can that hurt?"

"It wouldn't be one night for you. You'd want more."

True. So true. Deep down, she hoped Hunter would be so enthralled by her that he'd become addicted to her touch. "If he doesn't want me after the potion, I'll take a blood oath never to speak to him again." A small lie, really, since she only planned to leave out one word. Never.

"Sorry."

"Please. I'll bake those eye of newt muffins you love so much."

"Oh, you bitch. I love those." Several minutes passed in thick, brooding silence, before she shook her head. "Nope, sorry. I simply can't allow you to endure more hurt because of him."

"I'll wreak vengeance upon your greatest enemy. I'll go total witch on their ass."

Glory opened her mouth, then closed it with a snap. Opened. Closed. Her hazel eyes gleamed hopefully, glowing with otherworldly power like they did just before a spell. "Horrible, painful vengeance?"

"Yes."

"Even if it's, say, against Falon Ryis?"

"Hunter's best friend? *He's* your greatest enemy?" Genevieve blinked in surprise. "I didn't know you and Falon had even spoken to each other. Ever."

Glory's jaw clenched stubbornly. "I'm not going to explain. You make his life miserable, I'll give you the potion. Take it or leave it."

She didn't have to think about her answer. "I'll take it."

Glory slowly smiled. "Then the potion is yours."

"Thank you, thank you!" With a joyous whoop, she threw her arms around her sister. Sometimes family was a wonderful thing.

"What's going on in there?" Godiva called.

Glory said, "Genevieve accidentally conjured a male stripper, and we're placing dollar bills in his G-string. Just ignore us."

"Ha, ha. Very funny," came the muffled reply. Then, "I'll be there in a sec."

"Come on." Glory extracted herself from the bear hug and flounced down the candlelit hall, through thickly painted shadows, toward their bedrooms. "It's in my room. I really hope you know what you're doing," she murmured.

Did she? Genevieve mused. Not really. Did she care? Hell, no. Thoughts of lying naked in Hunter's arms eclipsed all else. He'd trace his fingers over her breasts, roll her nipples between his fingers. He'd kiss a path down her stomach, lingering, licking . . . "Uh, can we put a rush order on that potion?"

Glory unlocked her door with a quietly muttered "Open" and a wave of her delicate hand. Instantly the thin slab of wood creaked open. They stepped inside the room.

Genevieve's jaw nearly hit the ground. She rarely ventured in there and was momentarily shocked by the total chaos. Clothes and empty food cartons were scattered all over the floor, a sea of reds, blues, greens, and sweet and sour chicken orange.

"I need a minute," Glory said, already tossing shoes and other items aside as she scrounged through the mess.

"No, you need a maid." She pinched the 38D bra hanging from the lampshade between her fingers before dropping it on top of the matching panties at her feet.

"I've been depressed and haven't cleaned. Big deal." Pause. "Ah-ha! I found you, you little sneak." Smiling, Glory jumped up. A red bottle dangled from her fingers. "Love potion number thirteen."

Genevieve frowned. "I want love potion number nine."

"Trust me. Nine sucks. You want to ride a man like a bronco at peak rodeo season, you go with thirteen."

"I'll take it." Genevieve grabbed the crimson container and gently rolled it between her fingers. Dark liquid swirled inside, mesmerizing her. This was it, the answer to her prayers. Her heart drummed in her chest, faster, faster, then skipped a beat. This innocent-looking bottle was about to gift her with the best night of her life. Eager to begin, she reached for the cork, but her sister's next words stilled her hand.

"Drink half just before you walk into the bar, not a moment sooner. Only half. Understand?" Urgency rang from her voice like a clarion of bells.

"Yes. Why?"

"Uh, hello. You'll have every man in Mysteria following you and fighting for your attention if you drink it now. And the full bottle will cause . . . too much passion in you. Now go. Get out of here before I change my mind."

Genevieve needed no further prompting. "I love you." She kissed her sister's cheek and raced to her room. Quickly she changed into the sluttiest outfit she possessed. A black dress with a V neck so low it nearly touched her navel. The hem dangled mere inches below the curve of her ass. A little uncomfortable with the amount of skin showing, she slipped on a pair of tall hooker boots that hit just above her knees.

She left her hair down, the brunette tresses hanging along the curve of her back in sexy disarray. She spritzed jasmine perfume between her breasts and swiped do-me-hard red gloss over her lips. There. Done.

After grabbing a quarter, she grabbed her broom and skipped outside. Flying would be faster than driving. A cool night breeze kissed every inch of visible flesh—and boy, was there a lot of it. Amid the romantic haze of moonlight, insects sang a welcoming chorus, interspersed prettily with the buzz of fairy wings. Once she'd settled on top of the skinny broom handle, careful to cover her butt so she didn't moon the entire town, she commanded the contraption to fly.

"High, high my stead will soar. Touch the ground we shall no more." As the words left her mouth, the broom inched higher and higher into the air, then sped forward, moving faster than any car. Long tendrils of dark hair whipped her face, slapping her cheeks. Plumes of pink pollen whizzed past her, leaving behind an erotic scent.

When the lights of the town square came into view, framed by towering, majestic snowcapped mountains, she lowered and slowed. She stopped at the One-Stop Mart and bought a package of condoms from the pink-haired kid at the register. Outside, she popped back onto her broom and stuffed several foil wrappers in her dress.

Ever upward she soared again, past the tall pines. Whitewashed wooden buildings, dirt roads, and friendly people came into view, each weirder than the next. Psychics, vampires, trolls, fairies—Mysteria turned no one away.

As she flew over the town's wishing well, a lovely arching marble structure that glittered in the moonlight, she swooped low and dropped her quarter inside. "Let tonight be exciting," she said, wanting the wish to come true with every fiber of her being. Wisps of magic ribboned in the air, curling into the sky, making her shiver. She grinned.

Soon Knight Caps entered her line of vision, the tall stone structure bursting with people, laughter, and gyrating music. She slowed. Her heart raced when she finally stopped at the side of the building. Her palms began to sweat as she hovered, hidden by the shadows. What if Hunter was somehow able to resist the potion? She swallowed the sudden lump in her throat. What if she failed to attract him? What if—

Her teeth ground together. No. No thoughts of failure. Not tonight. Tonight wishes came true.

Stiffening her shoulders, she hopped to the ground. Her broom fell with a thump. Already she could sense Hunter's presence inside. His warm essence swirled around her, layered with a subtle fragrance of sex appeal and man. With shaky fingers, she studied the bottle one last time, only then seeing the warning label on the side.

"May cause dizziness," she read. "This drug may impair the ability to drive or operate machinery. Use care until you become familiar with its effects. Seek medical attention if liquid comes into contact with eyes."

Nothing she couldn't handle, she thought, popping the bottle's cork. "Bottom's up, Evie." She drained the contents. If half would make Hunter love her for a night, just think of what the full bottle could do. There was no such thing as too much passion. The bitter liquid tasted foul on her tongue, and she felt its quick descent into her stomach. Burning, burning. So hot. She coughed and doubled over. Her blood boiled, setting fire to everything inside her. She squeezed her eyes shut and tried to scream, but no sound emerged.

Thankfully the burning soon faded as if it had never been.

Blinking, Genevieve straightened and took stock of her physical being. She didn't *feel* any sexier. Didn't feel irresistible. Still, she inched to the front entrance. *I can do this. I'm a sexual cauldron of lust.* She pushed open the doors. *I'm a sexual cauldron of lust.* The sound of inane chatter and frantic music filled her ears. Smoke wafted around her, blending with the shadows and creating a dreamlike haze.

A small part of her expected everything male to attack her as her gaze searched the room for Hunter. No one paid her any heed. Where was—her heartbeat skidded to a stop. There he was. Behind the bar. For a moment, she forgot to breathe. He was serving drinks to a twittering, giggling fairy threesome. A rush of jealousy hit her. Each fairy possessed a startling, delicate beauty, with glittery skin and gossamer wings that entranced human men, bringing out their protective instincts. Not to mention lust. These fairies were completely pink, with fuchsia hair, rose skin, and seashell garments.

Hunter looked magnificent. His disheveled black hair tangled over his forehead and hit just below his ears. Silky. Tempting. His sharp cheekbones hinted at some foreign lineage. Probably royalty. A ruthless conqueror. His nose possessed an endearing bump and a scar nicked the right corner of his lips, most likely souvenirs from a barroom brawl.

He was probably six-foot-five, a veritable giant to her five-four. Obviously he worked out. A lot. His delicious biceps stretched the fabric of his black T-shirt. Overall (and quite surprisingly) he was not a handsome man. He was too savage looking. *Predator*, his mesmerizing green eyes proclaimed. An irresistible proclamation. She wasn't sure why he'd come to Mysteria, or what made him so different from other males that she had to have him. Only him.

He laughed at something one of the stupid flirting fairies said, and her jaw clenched. He must have sensed her presence in that moment because even as he laughed, his gaze traveled across the distance and locked on her. His smile grew even wider, and he waved in a welcome—until he saw her outfit. His eyes, suddenly blazing with fire, narrowed. His smile faded into a fierce frown; his hand fell to his side.

He turned away from her.

Oh, no no no. There would be no ignoring her tonight. No giving her the cold shoulder. *I'm a sexual cauldron of lust*, she thought, stepping into the bar.

· Two ·

I'M *dead*, Hunter Knight thought. *So freaking dead.*

His blood heated as his gaze drank in the vision that was Genevieve Tawdry. Actually, he didn't have to look at her to know her appearance. He'd memorized it long ago. Long, dark brown hair that glinted red in sunlight framed a serious little face. Pert nose, huge hazel eyes that sometimes glowed and were always fringed by the prettiest lashes he'd ever seen.

As usual, she mesmerized him.

Right now, in the dim strobe light of the bar, she appeared lovelier than ever. Her barely-there dress—holy hell, she might as well have been naked. Every muscle in his body (even his favorite) hardened to the point of pain. A pair of black boots stretched up her calves, just past her knees, leaving several inches of delicious thigh visible. Cleavage spilled from the deep V of her top. *Come over here and lick me*, that cleavage said.

What he would have given to take that cleavage up on its offer.

Every time he saw this woman, he experienced an inexorable urge to strip her and ride her. Hard. Ride her till she screamed his name. Ride her till she spasmed around his cock. Now was no different. Her slender body, with its hide-and-seek curves, would fit perfectly against him. Over him. Under him.

His teeth ground together. He wanted her desperately. He'd always wanted her.

And there was no way in hell he could have her.

Loving Genevieve would destroy him. Literally. Being psychic sucked ass. One touch of Genevieve's lips at their first meeting and he'd known, *known*, she would somehow kill him if he let himself get involved with her romantically.

That didn't stop the cravings, however, didn't stop her image from constantly haunting his dreams. Hell, in that scrap of black material she now wore, she might very well cause his heart to stop or his dick to explode.

"Hunter, will you get me a sex on the beach?" a high-pitched female voice said in front of him. Fairy laughter erupted, ringing like dainty bells.

He forced his gaze away from Genevieve, forced his lips to edge into a semblance of a smile, and met the impish gaze of one of the fairies. "Sure thing, sugar. Sex on the beach, just for you. I'll even add Knight's special ingredient."

More giggling. The girlish sound grated on his every nerve.

He thought he might have slept with one of these horny pixies (maybe all of them?) at some point last year, but at that moment he couldn't remember when. Or who. Or if they'd had a good time. He didn't care anymore. Couldn't get hard unless he thought of Genevieve.

What was it about her that so obsessed him? She was pretty, but other women were prettier. Maybe it was her amazing smell. No one smelled as sweet and intoxicating as Genevieve. Or maybe it was her eyes, so vulnerable. So determined.

He mixed the requested drink and slid it across the counter. From the corner of his eye he watched Genevieve saunter to the bar, her hips swaying seductively. She eased onto a stool, mere inches from his reach. Every nerve ending inside him leaped to instant life, clamoring for her. A touch, a press. Something. Anything.

"I'll have a flaming fairy," she said. Her voice dipped huskily, soft and alluring. Menacing.

The fairies gasped at the implied threat.

His lips twitched. Genevieve arched her brows—they were two shades darker than her hair, nearly black—silently daring the fairies to comment. They remained silent. He watched the byplay in amusement, admiring Genevieve's spirit and strength. Fairies were delicate creatures, at times human in size, at others merely flickering pinpricks of light. They adored sex and alcohol, gaiety and games, but they rarely fought. Most resided in the surrounding forest and Colorado mountains, visiting Mysteria when they grew bored.

"Are you refusing to serve me?" Genevieve asked him.

"Of course not," he said, realizing he hadn't moved an inch since she'd requested her drink. He grabbed a glass. He didn't allow himself to look at her and the tempting cleavage she displayed. Lately it was becoming harder and harder (literally!) to send her away.

Maybe he should not have cultivated a friendship with her, but he'd been unable to completely push her out of his life. He just, well, he wanted to spend time with her. She amused and exhilarated him.

At least she hadn't killed him. Yet.

Every time he saw her, he asked himself a single question: is she worth dying for? Always the answer was the same. No. No, she wasn't. Not then, not now. He might crave her, he might enjoy her, but he would *not* die for her. He lifted a bottle of rum.

"Sooo . . . how are you, Hunter?" she asked him.

Stay strong, he mentally chanted. *Fight her appeal.* But damn it all to hell, the urge to wrap her in his arms and give them both what they wanted was stronger tonight than ever before. "I'm good. Busy, though. I really need to see to my other customers. You'll have to excuse me."

He turned his back on her.

Silence.

Horrible, guilty silence where everything faded from his mind except the look of pain that passed over Genevieve's face. He wished he could take back the words and say something else. Something innocent like, You look nice. Something honest like, It's great to see you. As it was, hurt radiated from her and that hurt sliced through him sharper than any knife.

"Genevieve," he said, then pressed his lips together. If he told her he was sorry, he'd only be encouraging her.

"I still need my drink."

"Of course." Well, hell. He didn't know how to handle her anymore. Always his resolve teetered on the brink of total destruction—now even more so. He needed to send her away, but he wanted her to stay so badly. *She's not worth dying for, remember?*

He inhaled deeply, meaning to relax himself, but her scent filled him. More decadent than ever before. Pure temptation. Forbidden desire. Total seduction. Hot and wild. His eyelids closed of their own accord, and his hands ceased all movement, her drink once again forgotten.

"Hunter?"

His cock jumped, hardening further. Again, his name coming from her lush made-for-sin lips was torture. Too easily could he imagine her screaming his name while he pounded in and out of her.

Snap out of it, asshole, and fix her drink.

Hunter pried his eyes open and mixed vodka, peach schnapps, and cranberry, orange, and pineapple juices into the rum. Without ever glancing in her direction, he struck a match and lit the top on fire. Yellow-gold flames licked the rim of the glass before dying a hasty death. He slid the drink to Genevieve and turned away.

"What do I owe you?" she said in that breathy voice.

"You're my *friend*." They both needed the reminder. "It's on the house." If her fingertips brushed his while she handed him money, he'd come right then, right there. And he'd be willing to bet it would be the best orgasm of his life, no penetration required.

"Falon," Hunter called. Falon, his employee and best friend, was busy cleaning tables, but the tall, muscled male sauntered to the bar.

"Yeah?" Falon smiled a mysterious smile.

The three fairies trembled in reverence, bowing their heads in acknowledgment.

Falon had uptilted violet eyes, perfect white teeth, tanned skin that sometimes shimmered like it had been sprinkled with glitter, and shoulder-length blond hair with a slight wave. While human women lusted for him, fairy females were awed by him. They treated him as if he were a king, a god. Hunter had no idea why. Every time he asked, Falon shrugged and changed the subject.

Falon wasn't human, Hunter knew that, but he didn't

know exactly what type of creature Falon was. There was an unspoken rule in Mysteria: if you can't tell, don't ask.

"Do you mind taking over?" Hunter asked him. "I've, uh, decided to call it a night."

"I don't mind at all. I like the view from the bar." Falon's gaze strayed meaningfully to Genevieve. "I've been meaning to call Genevieve, anyway. So this works out perfectly."

Falon and Genevieve? Hunter froze in place, lances of possessiveness and jealousy blending together and spearing him. *Nothing you can do about it, man. Leave. Now.* Muscles clenched tightly, he strode toward the storeroom. His home was above the bar, and the only door to the staircase was there. He'd go upstairs and seduce a few bottles of Jack Daniel's. Maybe then he could wipe Genevieve's image from his mind. Not to mention the hated image of Genevieve and Falon.

"Thanks a lot, Tawdry," he heard one of the fairies murmur. "You scared Hunter away, just like you always do."

Genevieve growled. "If your greatest wish is to be bitch-slapped, color me Genie in a Bottle because I'm about to grant it."

Hearing the embarrassment in her tone and the shame she tried so hard to hide behind bravado, he stilled. Another wave of guilt washed through him. He'd rejected this woman at every turn. He'd embarrassed her in front of the entire town more times than he could count. And she'd never been anything but sweet to him.

He knew she was shy around men. The way her cheeks pinkened, the way she sometimes stumbled over her words and gazed at anything but him, proved that. Yet she'd worked up the courage to approach him time and time again. How could he hurt her yet again?

"I, for one, am glad Hunter left," Falon said, his tone seductive. "I've wanted to get Genevieve alone for a long time."

Get her alone? That poaching bastard. *Stop. Don't think like that.* Hunter rolled his shoulders and drew in a deliberate breath. Still, the thought of Falon and Genevieve together flashed through his mind again, the two of them naked and writhing. Rage seethed below the surface of his skin.

Maybe his psychic abilities were wrong. Maybe Genevieve wouldn't be the death of him. Maybe— He ran his tongue over his teeth. His instincts were never wrong, and he knew better than to fool himself into believing a lie. He had to keep pushing her away.

Except, pushing her away might send her straight into another man's arms. Something he'd always feared.

Yes, he'd always dreaded the day she would *stop* coming to him. That would mean she was ready to move on and accept another man. His hands fisted at his sides. He hadn't meant to, but he'd cultivated a tentative friendship with her to keep such a thing from happening. Was it wrong of him? Yes. Did he care? Hell, no. The idea of her with another man always blackened his mood and set him on killing edge.

If she went to someone else tonight, to Falon, he'd—he'd—no way in hell he was letting that happen, he decided.

Determination rushing through him, he spun on his heel. Genevieve still sat at the bar, her shoulders hunched, her face lowered toward her empty glass as Falon spoke to her. Her hair tumbled over her shoulders, shielding her delectable cleavage.

"Genevieve," he called before he could stop himself.

The music skidded to a halt, the band members too interested in what was happening to play. In fact, everyone present went silent and locked eyes on him. Everyone except Genevieve, that is. She continued to stare into her glass, her gaze faraway, lost.

"Genevieve, you beautiful thing, I need your attention."

Finally her chin snapped up and she faced him, shock filling her luscious hazel eyes. "Did you say beautiful? Are you talking to me?"

"Is your name Genevieve?"

"Well, yes."

Oh, how she enticed him. She was all innocence, yet she possessed a wild, sex-kitten allure. It was a lethal, contradictory combination that always intrigued him. "Why don't you have a seat at one of the tables, and I'll join you in a minute."

"Thanks a lot, Hunter," Falon said, but there was a glimmer of amusement in his tone. Scamming bastard.

Genevieve's nose crinkled and her brow furrowed, the planes of her face darkening with suspicion. "Why?"

"Because."

"That's not an answer. What do you want to talk about?"

He flicked a pointed glance to their avid audience. "It's private."

"I don't understand." Then her lips—her lush, kiss me, lick me all over, do-me-all-night lips—pressed together. Comprehension dawned in her eyes. She smiled slowly, seductively, yet somehow she appeared even more sad.

Now *he* was the one confused. What had made her happy and sad all at once? What did she comprehend?

"I would love to 'talk' with you," she said.

He gulped. She made it sound like they'd be going at it like wild animals on the tabletop. Maybe they would. If only she didn't tempt him on every level. Why did the Fates have to be so cruel? He desired this woman desperately, but he couldn't have her as anything more than a friend.

She eased to her feet, and he choked back a laugh when she flipped the rose-colored pixies off. His laugh died a sudden death when he saw that her dress barely fell below the curve of her bottom. His fingers itched to touch.

None of the tables were empty. Everyone watched her curiously as she crossed her arms over her chest. "You have five seconds to give me a table or I'll conjure your spouses into the bar. They'll find out what you've been doing and—"

Before the last word emerged, everyone at the tables jolted

to their feet—everyone except Barnabas Vlad, the art gallery owner. He didn't have a spouse. Chairs skidded, drinks sloshed over rims. "Here, take mine," rose in disharmony. Satisfied, Genevieve skipped to the table hidden in the corner, partially covered in a shadowy haven. "I'll take yours, John Foster. Thank you."

The town pervert was too busy staring at her cleavage to respond.

"Move out of her damn way!" Hunter shouted.

John nearly jumped out of his skin as he leaped away from Genevieve.

"And play some music. *Now.*" Hunter scowled at the band leader. "That's what I pay you for, isn't it?"

A few seconds later, soft, romantic music drifted from the speakers. His scowl deepened. Resisting Genevieve was hard enough; throw in a romantic atmosphere . . . heaven help him.

The three fairies were frowning, he noticed, and Falon was leaning his hip against the bar. "You're putting on quite a show tonight," his friend said.

"I'm glad you find it entertaining." He paused, looked away. "I'm taking a break."

"That's nice."

"You're still in charge."

"That's nice, too."

"Yeah, well, you're an asshole and if you don't wipe that smirk off your face, you're fired."

Falon's deep laughter followed him as he stormed to Genevieve's table and plopped down across from her. Once again, her delicious scent enveloped him. He shouldn't have instigated this, but now that he had he was helpless to stop.

"What did you want to talk about?" She propped her elbows on the table and leaned forward, granting him another spectacular view. Sweet heaven above, she wasn't wearing a bra.

Had he suggested they talk? Perhaps a better suggestion would be that he shoot himself here and now and just get his death over with. "We've known each other a long time," he began, fighting past the friction of sexual need working through him.

"Yes."

"And we've never discussed—" What the hell was a safe, nonsexual topic?

"Yes?" she prompted, grinning.

Her teeth were two rows of pearly white perfection. And she had a dimple. Why had he never noticed it before? *Probably because you've rarely given her a reason to smile at you, moron.* He yearned to nibble on the delectable little morsel.

"We've never discussed—" He paused yet again. The weather? No, he'd only picture her naked in the rain. Favorite places to shop? No, he'd picture her shopping naked. Favorite books? No, he'd picture her reading naked.

Ah, hell.

Is she worth your life? Now, this moment, he couldn't say no so easily.

"There's got to be *something* you want to talk about." She licked her lips, her pink tongue as lethal as any weapon of mass destruction.

They could talk about taxes at this point and he'd be aroused. "I—how have you been doing lately?" he asked. He leaned as far back in the stool as he could, hoping distance would clear his foggy senses.

"Good."

"How are your sisters?"

"They're good." She tapped a finger to her chin, her oval nail glinting in the light. "Hunter, is there something else you want to say to me?"

He tangled a hand through his hair. Hell, yes, there was something he wanted to say to her: get naked.

How did she twist him into knots like this? He saw her, and he wanted her. He caught a whiff of her sweet fragrance, and he wanted her. He closed his eyes, and he wanted her.

Is she worth dying for?

He stared at her, watching the way shadows and light played across her lovely, serious little face. Watching the way hope flickered in her eyes, lighting the hazel to an otherworldly green.

Before the night was over, he was going to have this woman's thighs around his waist. Or head. He wasn't picky. He was going to know what it felt like to touch her curves, to know her taste. He was going to know how her expression changed when she climaxed. The future be damned.

Not giving himself time to consider the ramifications, he shoved to his feet and held out his hand, palm up. "Genevieve, would you please dance with me?"

"Really?" Disbelief and awe rained over her face before she frowned. "You don't plan to leave me in the middle of the song, do you?"

His chest constricted. He'd done that to her on numerous occasions. In his defense, he'd become so aroused holding her in the curve of his body he'd had two choices: leave her on the dance floor or screw her on the dance floor. "We'll dance the entire song. I promise."

Slowly she grinned. "Yes. Yes. I would love to dance with you."

The moment she placed her fingers atop his, his senses screamed with approaching danger. He ignored the warning. Here, in this moment, nothing mattered except cherishing Genevieve the way he'd yearned to cherish her all these many years.

Was she worth dying for?

Hell, yes.

· Three ·

OH, wonder of wonders, it had worked! The love potion had actually worked.

Her hand in his, Hunter led her onto the dance floor. Where their skin touched, she tingled. He'd asked to do this; he'd even said please. She hadn't begged—not that she would have. (Okay, she might have.)

They stopped in the center of the floor, paused for a moment, facing and watching each other. Their breath intermingled—his was shallow, hers was coming in fast, erratic pants. Multihued light pulsed from the strobe above, caressing his face, and music flowed seductively.

Something she'd never seen before flittered over his expression. Something infinitely tender. Her stomach flip-flopped. What thoughts were rolling through his mind? He reached out and sifted a strand of her hair between his fingers, then brushed it from her temple. His touch electrified her.

The need to breathe was forgotten. Only Hunter existed, only Hunter mattered. His fingers slid down her shoulders, along her arms, and circled her waist. Her lips parted on a sudden gasp of pleasure. His strong arms locked around her, gathering her close. Heat zinged and crested, then his hands were anchored on her lower back.

"Hunter," she said, unsure why she'd whispered his name. It was there, in her mind, in her blood, branded on her cells.

"Genevieve," he returned softly. "So lovely."

Throughout the years, she'd prayed he would accept what was between them. She would have prayed even harder if she'd known the sheer magnificence reality would be. Her chest pressed to his, nipples hard and aching; his strength seeped through her scanty dress. And he didn't jerk away from her, didn't run. The scent of him, heat and man, enveloped her.

Together they swayed to the erotic rhythm of the music. Several times, his erection brushed against her. Delicious. Welcome. Their gazes never strayed. Constantly sizzled.

Emboldened, she rasped her hands up the buttery soft material of his T-shirt. He sucked in a sharp breath. "I've wanted to be your lover for so long," she admitted.

"I've wanted that, too. So badly."

Her fingers played with the hair at his neck. "Some days

I would have sworn you desired me. Some days I would have sworn you hated me."

"I always desired you. You're total pleasure, sweetheart." He paused. Frowned. "You're eternity."

Eternity . . . With that one word, joy and sadness battled for supremacy inside her. Joy because he was talking about forever with her; sadness because it had taken a love potion to get him to this point. However, she shoved the sadness away. Tonight was a night for magic and love. She would allow nothing else to intrude.

Tomorrow the sadness could return and erode the precious memories she had formed. As for now, she would take what she could get, however she could get it.

She'd wanted him too long.

"I'll give you eternity," she said. "I'll give you anything you ask for."

He broke eye contact and pulled her the rest of the way into his body. Her head rested on the hollow of his shoulder. "I've watched you grow from pretty teenager to exquisite woman."

A shiver stole over her skin. Was he speaking true, or did the love potion beckon him to lie and say anything that might please her? "Why did you constantly push me away, then?"

He ignored her question. "Every time you walked into a room, you consumed my attention. If you had known just how much I desired you, you would have pursued me all the more. And if you'd pursued me any more, I wouldn't have been able to resist you."

Sparks of exotic sensation pulsed through her. Unable to help herself and craving the taste of him, she grazed her lips over his neck. Her hands clutched at his back. Mmm, his skin tasted good, like expensive wine and twilight magic.

"There was no reason to resist me," she said. "I wanted to be with you."

"You amaze me." He nuzzled her nose. "You could have any man you want, but you never gave up on me."

That sad little gleam returned to her eyes, and Hunter knew he'd do anything to get rid of it. "What if I swore to never run from you again? Would you smile for me?"

In lieu of an answer, she brushed her lips over his neck once more. This time, however, she let her tongue explore, twirling, circling. He cupped her butt, lifting her slightly, and his erection rubbed the crevice between her legs. A moan tore from her. They were fully clothed, yet they were managing to make love on the dance floor, despite the people circling them.

Genevieve bit his ear. "Help me understand why you ran. Did you think I would use you? Did you think we would no longer be able to remain friends?"

He laughed, the sound devoid of humor. "No. I knew you wanted more than sex from me. I knew our friendship could survive."

"Then . . . why?"

"Genevieve," he said. The grief in her voice sliced through him, more lethal than a blade. He couldn't tell her the truth because it would frighten her away. If she knew she was going to be the death of him, she would leave him.

Now that he had her in his embrace, he wanted to keep her there. *Would* keep her there. He couldn't believe he'd pushed her away for so long. Stupid. A mistake he'd never make again. Never had a woman felt more perfect in his arms.

After all the years he'd hurt her, she deserved romance from him. Sweetness, tenderness, more than he'd ever given another.

"You have the most amazingly expressive eyes." He allowed his fingers to crawl down the curve of her bottom and play with the hem of her dress. "Have I ever told you that?"

She sucked in a gasp of air; then, as she released the breath, she relaxed against him fully. "No. You never told me."

"More fool me. Your eyes are so intoxicating, sometimes green, sometimes velvety brown, and I always feel like I'm lost in them." He brushed the side of her face with his, tickling her softness with his slight beard stubble, relishing the contact. He kissed the tip of her nose. Not dipping lower and tasting her lips proved nearly impossible. "Did you know you have three faint little freckles on your nose? When you're angry or sad, those freckles darken. I've wondered over and over again if you have freckles on the rest of your body."

"I could . . ." She gulped. Her eyes widened and filled with eagerness. "I could show you."

"Yes. I would love that." *I'm not an honorable man*. He stilled with the thought. Here she was, offering him a paradise he didn't deserve. His mouth curled into a frown, and he stared down at her. She deserved a man who could love her forever, a man who hadn't hurt her for years.

So what? he thought in the next instant. She wanted him; he wanted her. He wasn't a martyr. For what short time they had together—he knew his death was certain now, but he was past the point of caring—he would give her everything. His heart, his attention, his affection. He'd love her so thoroughly she'd savor the memories for the rest of her life.

"I truly am sorry for how I've treated you in the past, sweetheart."

"I forgive you," she said, her features sincere.

His brows arched in surprise. "That easily?"

"We're friends, aren't we?"

"Genevieve." He groaned her name as he meshed his lips into hers. She immediately parted for him, welcoming him inside. Her decadent flavor filled his mouth, so much richer than he'd ever imagined. She moaned, a needy sound, a greedy sound.

Urgency roared to intense life. Shards of her magic flowed into his cells, awakening pieces of him he hadn't known existed, crowning him with power and vitality. Warming him.

He felt the pinprick rasps of her nipples against his chest and had to clench his fists in the material of her skirt to keep from kneading her breasts. Had they been anywhere else but a crowded barroom, he would have taken her. Would have pushed them both over the sweet edge of seduction.

"I want you," she breathed. "I want to make love with you."

"Hell, yes." He'd place her gently in his bed and smooth his hands over her. Work his way up and down her body with his tongue. Her legs would part, revealing the wetness of her arousal. "Stay the night with me." *Stay forever.*

"Yes. With all my heart, yes."

His cock jerked in reaction. Passion blazed in her eyes—passion for him. Only him. She smoothed her tongue over her lips, taking his taste with it. Her eyes closed in surrender, and she was the very picture of desire. Of lust and love and his most private dreams.

"Tell me what you're going to do with me, once you have me in bed," she said in a needy, aroused whisper. As if she had to know right then or she'd combust.

"What would you like me to do?" If he did half the things floating through his mind, they wouldn't walk for a week.

"Everything."

He rubbed against her, the action causing pleasure/pain flickers through his body. "Kiss you?"

"Mmm-hmm." She bit her bottom lip.

"Touch you?" He wanted so badly to drag her up to his room, to kiss and touch her *now*, but he was going to dance the entire song with her if it killed him. And it just might.

A tremor slipped down her spine. "Where would you touch me?"

"Everywhere."

Another tremor. "Yes, do that. Touch me everywhere."

"I'll taste you everywhere, too."

"Please, yes."

He licked the shell of her ear. "I'm going to make you come so many times, you'll—"

The double doors suddenly bounded open and a horde of . . . creatures burst inside the bar, surrounded by a palpable air of menace. Instinctively sensing their danger, Hunter shoved Genevieve behind his back. The music screeched to a halt. At the bar, the three fairies instantly shrunk to their tiniest size, puffs of glitter-smoke wafting from them.

Short, winged monsters with long fangs, more fur than a bear during hibernation, and razor-sharp claws formed a line in front of the doors, blocking escape. Their eyes were red and glowing; their angled, grotesque features were misshapen. Hideous.

They were subdemons, he realized.

Though different breeds were formed every day and he'd never encountered this type, Hunter recognized their scent: sulfur. As a monster hunter—pretending to be nothing more than a bar owner—he'd stalked and killed their kind most of his life. Demons, vampires, predators of the night—the scum of the earth, in his opinion. They were creatures who survived on human carnage. They were pure evil, and he despised them all.

Killing them had always been one of his favorite pastimes.

"Did someone wish for excitement?" one of them asked.

Genevieve gasped. "Oh, no. No, no. I take it back. No excitement."

"I suggest you leave," Hunter told them, the actual words nearly undetectable, laced with rage. Genevieve slipped her hand into his, and he felt a tremor rush through her. "Don't worry, sweetheart, I'll take care of this," he assured her quietly.

"No." The demon who had spoken, the tallest of the bunch—which wasn't saying much, since he only reached Hunter's navel—stepped forward and grinned slowly, anticipatingly. "I think we'll stay."

The grainy, high-pitched voice sent shudders through him. "Your kind isn't wanted here."

The creature's stance became cocky, arms crossed over his chest, legs slightly parted, his expression taunting. His dark, broken wings fluttered like an erratic heartbeat. "Your woman doesn't agree. She wished for excitement, so excitement we'll give her."

"I've changed my mind." Fighting past her fear, Genevieve stepped beside Hunter. She maintained her hold on him. Inside, her magic churned and swirled, dark and dangerous, ready for release. Sometimes the darkness of her powers frightened her more than her opponent; now she felt only fear for Hunter's safety. "He asked you to leave nicely. If you don't, I'll wreak such horrible vengeance upon you that you'll go home crying to the devil like little girls."

"We're not going anywhere until we've granted your wish. Master's orders." Laughing, the demons broke apart, knocking over tables, throwing chairs, climbing up and down the walls, and tearing off chunks of stone. Men and women, fairies and gnomes, gasped and raced (or flew) out of the way. That the gnomes, stumpy, trunklike monsters with more brawn than brain, were scared, added to her worries.

"Go upstairs and lock yourself in my room," Hunter demanded.

"I won't leave you to deal with them alone. I can make them go away." Amid shrieks of horror, the frantic pitter-patter of frightened people, and the evil vibrations of demon laughter, Genevieve raised her hands high in the air. "Burn to ash these demons shall, never a night again to prowl."

As she spoke, the demons flinched, anticipating the bombardment of her magic.

"Pain and suffering you will endure," she finished, "of this I am very sure."

Nothing happened.

Shocked, frowning, she tried again. Again, nothing.

The demons smiled slowly. "Looks like the witchy-poo has lost her powers."

More shock pounded through her; she uttered the spell for the third time. Still, no results. Why? "I—I don't understand." Why wouldn't her magic work? A side effect of the love potion? No, surely not, but Glory had told her to only drink half. The demons should be writhing balls of fire. Instead, they were chuckling and amused.

"Playtime is over," a grating voice proclaimed. The demon snarled and flashed his dripping fangs. "Get her!"

"Genevieve!" Hunter shouted as a creature lunged for her. Hunter grabbed it by the forearms and tossed it to the ground. He kicked and hit the demon with expert precision. His arms arched through the air so quickly the movements were barely visible. He ducked and spun, leaped and struck with poetic menace.

Falon joined the fray, stabbing at the monkey wannabes with broken liquor bottles and wood shards.

With the men occupied, another demon dove for her, slamming her into a table and knocking every ounce of air from her lungs. Dizzy, she sank to the ground. The only people she'd ever fought were her sisters, yet they hadn't wanted to actually kill her. Still, she knew the basics of self-defense and how to fight dirty.

Her opponent jumped astride her, pinning her where she lay. It licked its lips and tried to wrap its claws around her neck. She put her newly filed nails to use and poked it in the eyes. It howled, its attention on its pain, and she smashed her palm into its nose. In the next instant, Hunter kicked the demon away from her and grappled the hell spawn to the ground.

"Demons of the night," she chanted, standing, arms high in the air, "you will die now, I don't care how."

The fight continued without interruption.

Damn it! She glared down at her hands. Why wasn't her magic working? She felt the power of it inside her, as potent as ever, yet it refused to be released.

From the corner of her eye, she saw a demon's razor-sharp claws lengthen and slash at Hunter's chest. He didn't move in time, and blood began to ooze from the gaping wound. She gasped. Screamed. Fury and fear bubbled inside her.

"Run, baby," he panted, struggling to keep the creature from his throat.

"No, I won't leave you." Nearing panic, she grabbed a long, splintered wood shard and raced toward the battling pair just as Hunter punched the bastard in the face and rolled away. "Catch!" She tossed him the shard.

He caught it, and when the demon advanced, Hunter stabbed it dead center in the chest.

The creature burst into flames.

As the orange-gold flickers licked the walls and dissolved into ash, the tallest of the demons stopped tormenting a screaming gnome long enough to focus narrowed eyes on Hunter, who was pushing to his feet.

"You'll pay for that, human." Two other demons approached the leader's side, each of them glaring with hostility. "Oh, you'll pay."

Genevieve grabbed a beer bottle, broke the end on the bar, and held the jagged amber glass in front of her. "You'll have to fight me, as well," she said bravely. At least, she hoped she sounded brave.

"With pleasure, little witch," was the delighted reply.

"Damn it, Genevieve," Hunter said. "When this is over I'm going to teach you to obey my orders." He closed in on the demon, and a bleeding Falon closed into step at his side. Both men wore expressions of certain death—demon death.

Her heart drummed in her chest. *What should I do, what should I do, what should I do?* When she'd wished for excitement, she hadn't meant *this*.

Distracted as she was, she didn't notice as one of the demons sprinted to her. It reached her and knocked the glass from her hand before tossing her to the ground. Suddenly breathless, she lay still for a long while. Or perhaps she lay for mere seconds. Her attacker jumped on top of her and she fought like a wildcat, kicking and scratching. As it attempted to subdue her, its rancid breath fanned her face.

"Be still!" it hissed. Its forked tongue slithered from between thin lips.

She bit its arm, the taste of salt and ash filling her mouth.

"Bitch!"

"That's *witch* to you." She worked her arms free and clashed her hands together, then backhanded the creature across the face.

"Dead witch." Its sharp, lethal fangs emerged, dripping with . . . what? Not saliva. This smelled bad. Worse than bad. Evil. Like death. It gripped her wrists and held them down, its head inching toward her. She knew it was moving quickly, about to sink its fangs into her neck, but her mind processed it in slow motion.

She pulled her knees to her chest and slammed her feet into the demon's chest. Surprisingly, it flew backward and propelled across the bar. Gasping for air, trembling in fear, she jolted to a sitting position.

"You okay?" Hunter panted, at her side. He dropped to his knees. Sweat and blood dripped from his temples. His gaze roved over her body frantically, over her ripped dress, searching for injury.

"I'm fine. But you—"

"Look out!" Falon shouted.

Hunter whipped around; Genevieve gazed, horrified, past his shoulder. The demon she'd kicked was flying at her, hate in its eyes, a long shard of glass in its outstretched hand, mere seconds away from reaching her. Instinctively, she dove to the side. Anticipating such a move, the demon moved with her. Hunter, damn him, sprang in front of her, taking the blow himself.

"Hunter!" she screamed.

Eyes wide, he looked down at his chest.

"Got him." Laughing, the demon and the rest of his cohorts raced away. Some jumped through windows, the sound of tinkling glass echoing from the walls. Others rushed out the same way they'd entered. Hinges squeaked as the front doors burst into shattered pieces.

Genevieve's mind registered only one thing. "You're hurt. Hunter, you're hurt." Still on her knees, she scrambled in front of him. Blood dripped from his chest, the glass embedded so deeply she could only see the tip.

"I'll be fine." Weakness and pain tinged his voice. "Did they hurt you? Are you cut anywhere?"

"I'm okay, damn you. I'm okay." He looked so pale, causing her panic to intensify. Not even when she'd first spied the demons inside the bar had she felt this much fear. "You should have let him stab me." Her chin trembled. "You should have let him stab me."

"I'm glad you're well." His eyelids drifted shut for a long moment. "I'd have to become a ghost and do the revenge thing if they'd harmed you."

"I need to pull out the glass and bandage your wounds, okay? I need to—"

"It's too late. Demon saliva . . . is poison, and one of them managed to bite me. Genevieve," Hunter said, his voice so raspy she had trouble hearing him. "I want you . . . to know, you were totally . . . worth it."

Her arms anchored around him, her head burrowing against his chest. His heartbeat thumped weakly, sporadically. "Hunter, listen to me. You're going to be okay. Let's get you to my sister. She's a healer." She gazed at the bar, wild and desperate. "Someone call Godiva. Call her right now."

"I'll do it," Falon said.

"My head is spinning." Hunter's forehead bobbed forward. "Help me lie down, sweetheart."

His full weight fell into her. She absorbed it as best she could, locking one hand at the base of his neck and the other at his lower back. Leaning forward, she slowly and as gently as possible lowered him. Seconds dragged by. By the time he lay completely prone, her arms burned and shook with exertion.

"I wish I could have had more time with you," he said. He didn't open his eyes. "That's my only regret."

"Stop. Don't talk like that. You're going to be fine." Her chin trembled all the harder; her blood ran cold. She tore the shirt from his chest and studied the rest of his wounds. What she saw made her mouth dry up. Long, jagged scratches ran like bloody rivers over his ribs. Several teeth marks adorned his neck, the skin already black. Already dead.

She covered her mouth with her hand to cut off her horrified cry. "I love you, and I need you. Tell me you're going to be okay."

His lips lifted in a weak smile. "I wish . . . I wish . . ." As his voice tapered to quiet, his head drifted to the side.

Genevieve screamed. “No.” She gripped his shoulders and shook him. “You’re going to be okay. You’re going to be okay.” Violently, she continued to shake him. “Open your eyes, damn it. Open them right now or I’ll curse you to live in a monastery.”

He didn’t respond.

Falon approached slowly and crouched down. He reached out and placed two fingers over Hunter’s neck. Tears filled his eyes. “I’m sorry, Genevieve, but he was dead the second the demon bit him. They produce a poison that no human can survive.”

“No. No. When my sisters get here, we’ll cast a spell and he’ll be fine. You’ll see. He’ll be fine.” A huge lump formed in her throat, making it difficult to breathe. “He’s going to be fine,” she whispered raggedly, more for herself than Falon.

Yet even after she and her sisters cast their spells, Hunter remained motionless. Lifeless. Dead.

Yes, Hunter Knight was dead. And there wasn’t a damn thing she could do about it.

Four

"Uh, Mr. Collins. I think you should know something."

Roger Collins, owner and operator of Mysteria Mortuary—as well as a closet shape-shifter (spotted owl)—looked up from his desk and faced his apprentice, a freckle-faced boy with a pasty, almost gray complexion. "What's happened, hoo hoo, now?"

"Hunter Knight's body has disappeared."

Exasperated, Roger scratched his shoulder with his nose. Things like this were always happening, and he was tired of it. "Let's keep this between us, hoo hoo. No reason to alert the town." They'd only cancel the burial, and he'd be out a hefty chunk of change. No thanks. "Knight's funeral, hoo hoo, will happen as scheduled."

"HUUUNNNTERRRRR. Hunter Knight, you silly boy. Wake up, *s'il vous plait.*"

The voice called to him from a long, dark tunnel. Hunter tried to blink open his eyes, but it hurt too badly so he left them shut. Did lead weights hold the lids down? His mouth was dry, and his limbs were weak. Most of all, his neck throbbed.

What had happened to him?

He remembered fighting the demons, remembered Genevieve leaning over him. Remembered a black shadow swooping him up and carrying him away. And then, nothing. He remembered nothing after that.

"*Mon dieu!* Aren't you just the prettiest little thing." A soft hand smoothed over his brow. "I could snack on you all day and come back for leftovers."

That hand . . . His ears twitched. He could hear the rush of blood underneath the surface of skin. He could even hear the faint *thump, thump* of a heart. His mouth suddenly flooded with moisture. Hungry, he realized. He was so hungry he could have gnawed off his own arm.

"Well, don't just lie there. I know you're awake. Pay some attention to *moi*, you naughty boy. I saved your life, after all." A pause. "Well . . . I kind of saved your life. Maybe a more truthful saying would be I saved your death."

The voice was deep enough that he knew it belonged to

a man, but it was surprisingly feminine. And that horrible French accent . . . Despite the pain, Hunter forced his eyelids apart. Dank blackness greeted him. But slowly, very slowly his eyes adjusted, and he was able to make out a rocky cavern and a silhouette. The silhouette became a body . . . the body became a man . . . and then he saw everything as clearly as if the sun were shining.

"Hello, my little love puppet," the man said. "We're going to have *the* best eternity together, *oui*."

"Barnabas?" Hunter asked, rubbing his eyes.

"None other," he said with a proud lift of his chin.

Barnabas Vlad, owner of Mysteria's only art gallery ("art," of course, meaning pornographic photos); Hunter had come across the man only a few times. Last time he'd seen him, the man had been inside the bar. Something about him had always set Hunter's nerves on edge—something besides the fact that Barnabas often hit on him like a sailor on leave.

Right now Barnabas was dressed in a black, Oriental-styled gown, and he twirled a black parasol in his hand. Usually he wore huge blue sunglasses, but he wasn't wearing those now.

His eyes glowed bright red.

Hunter jumped to his feet, behind the stone dais he had lain upon. He winced in pain, but held his ground. "You're a vampire." He spat the word, for it was a foul curse to him.

"*Oui, oui.*" Barnabas's glossed lips stretched into a

happy, unconcerned smile. "What do you think of my outfit? It's new. Very *china doll* meets *modern society*, don't you think?"

"I think your dress needs a hole in it," Hunter snarled. "Right in the vicinity of your undead heart." His gaze circled the cavern, searching for anything he could use as a stake. There were no rocks, no twigs. Damn it. What he would have given for his COTN—creatures of the night—arsenal at home.

"Why are you looking at me like that?" Barnabas's smile became a pout, and he splayed his arms wide. "You're a vampire, too, *mon ami*."

"No, I'm not."

"*Oui*, you are."

"No, I'm not."

"*Oui*, you are."

"No. I'm. Not. I'm a vampire *hunter*, you disgusting, vile, rotten piece of dog shit."

Barnabas took no offense and laughed, actually laughed. "Not anymore. Feel your neck. I drained your blood and gave you mine."

There was truth in the vampire's expression, truth and utter enjoyment. Everything inside Hunter froze. No. No! He couldn't be a vampire. He'd rather die.

Hesitant, hand shaky, Hunter reached up. He could taste blood in his mouth, it was true, but the rest . . . His fingertips brushed over the small, very real puncture wounds on the side of his neck. He knew exactly what that meant. *No*, he thought again. He hunted vampires; he hated them. Before Genevieve, it had been his only purpose in life. "Now . . . you putrid sack of undead flesh." Glaring, he pointed a finger at Barnabas, wishing it were a stake. "Why would you make me a vampire? Why didn't you let me die?"

With a guilty flush, Barnabas hopped onto the dais. "I was in the bar the night those demons attacked you. When you fell, you were covered in blood and, *mon dieu*, you looked so tasty. I didn't cop a feel or anything, if that's what has you so worried."

"That's not what I'm worried about," he shouted. *I'm a monster now. I'm the very thing I despise.* He knew a lot about vampires. They were—had been—his business, after all, and he'd seen many people make the change from human to beast. Oh, they tried to fight the urge to drink.

They never won.

Always the thirst for blood, for life, seduced and consumed them. They killed the people they once loved—and everyone else around them. *I can never allow myself to see Genevieve again.* The wretched thought nearly dropped him to his knees. Nearly felled him.

Barnabas has lived in Mysteria for a long time, and he hasn't slaughtered the population. Hunter paused, blinked. How seductive the thought was and he grasped onto it with desperation. Maybe he was wrong about vampires. Maybe vampires didn't kill—

He squeezed his eyes closed. Such rationalizations were dangerous and could get Genevieve slain. No, he couldn't see her, couldn't risk it.

"Are you worried that you will no longer have a sexual appetite? You will, I assure you." The vampire's eyes stroked over him, stripped him, glowing a brighter red with every second that passed. "Despite the myths, you will function as you always did—except for the sunlight thing and the blood thing. Small prices to pay, really."

"Considering what?" he snarled. "There are no advantages that I can see."

"There are most certainly advantages." Barnabas tapped a black-gloved finger onto his chin. "You'll get stronger every day. Faster. You'll be a force no man—uh, woman—can resist. Like *moi*. After a while, you'll even enjoy taking blood. I pinky promise."

"I'll be a killer." This wasn't happening, couldn't possibly be happening. He tangled a hand through his hair.

"You won't be a killer."

"Yes, I will."

"*Mais non*, you won't."

"Yes. I. Will. Your continued arguing is really starting to piss me off."

"Do you want to fight me?" Barnabas asked hopefully. "I'm always up for naked wrestling."

Hunter bared his teeth in a scowl. As he did so, his incisors elongated. He actually felt them do it, sliding down, sharpening. He smelled the metallic twang of blood in the air—blood from a recent feeding Barnabas had enjoyed. How thirsty Hunter suddenly was. He shook with the force of it. "I can't drink blood. I just can't."

"You smell me, don't you? You want to sink your teeth into me? Go ahead. I already gave you blood, but you were asleep and didn't get to taste the sweetness of it." Barnabas motioned him over with a wave of his hand. "Taste it. You might like it. But you had better hurry. Soon my heart will shrivel up again, the blood gone, and there'll be nothing left for you to taste."

Hunter's stomach twisted in revulsion—and eagerness. He found himself stepping toward Barnabas, closing the distance between them, unable to stop himself. He found himself leaning down, teeth bared, mouth watering.

Genevieve's beautiful image flashed inside his mind. *She's in trouble.* The knowledge flooded him, his psychic ability attuned to her. Even in death. He straightened with a jolt. Blood was forgotten. Only Genevieve mattered. "Show me the way out of this cave before I kill you, vampire." He'd save her, then leave her.

Barnabas frowned. "You're not ready to leave."

"Yes, I am."

"*Mais non*, you're not."

"Yes, I am. And you're not French, so stop with the accent."

"I haven't taught you the way of our kind yet."

Rage poured through him as if he'd drunk it. "*Your* kind, vampire. I will never be like you."

"*Oui*, you will."

"No. I. Won't. Stop arguing. My woman is in trouble, and I *will* save her."

"Fine. Go. I've already fed you, so you don't have to worry about drinking for a while yet." Barnabas's eyes flashed red with jealousy. "But when the hunger hits you, you'll come back to me. I know you will."

"SHE hasn't stopped crying for three days."

"She refuses to eat. She barely has the energy to sit up and drink the water I force down her."

"What should we do?"

"I don't know. I just . . . I don't know."

Genevieve heard her sisters' hushed voices and stared up at the hole she'd blown in the ceiling yesterday. Why couldn't she have done that the night of the brawl? The morning after Hunter's death, her magic had returned to full operating capacity, but she hadn't needed it. And now she didn't care.

"Should we call a doctor?"

She rolled to her side, placing her back to her sisters. Why wouldn't they leave her alone? She just wanted peace—from their voices, from life. From the flashing, bloody images of Hunter's death.

"Genevieve, sweetie, we know you're awake. Talk to us," Godiva begged, her tone tinged with concern. The wolf she had saved plopped at her ankles and nudged her hand, wanting to be petted. "Tell us how we can help you."

"Bring Hunter back to life." Her throat ached from her crying. Raw, so raw. Like her spirit. "That's all I want."

"We can't do that," Glory said softly. "Raise his body from the ground, yes, but the risen dead become predators. Killers. You know that. The longer the dead walk the earth, the hungrier for life they become. He would eat you up and spit out your bones."

Yes, she knew that, but hearing it tore a sharp lance of pain through her. One moment she'd had everything she'd ever dreamed, the next she had only despair. *Hunter*, her heart cried.

"The surviving demons are destroying Mysteria," Godiva said. "We need your help to stop them."

"I can't." Strength had long since deserted her. More than that, any concern she'd had for the town and its citizens had died with Hunter. "I just can't."

Glory claimed her right side, and Godiva sat at her left. Surrounding her. "His funeral is today. Do you want to go?"

"No." She didn't want to see him inside a casket. A part of her wanted to pretend he was still alive, simply hiding somewhere. "Why did he have to die? Why? The love potion had worked. He wanted me as much as I wanted him."

"Uh, um." Glory looked away, at anything and everything but her sisters. "Humm."

Godiva's eyes narrowed. "What did you do, Glor?"

Pause.

"Glory!"

"Well, Evie asked for a love potion. I didn't think Hunter deserved her, and knew if he loved her for one night, then dumped her the next day, she'd be devastated."

"What did you do?" Godiva repeated.

Another pause.

"Don't make me ask again," Godiva said, raising her arms as if to cast a spell.

"I, uh, sort of gave her a power depressant instead."

"Sort of?"

"Okay, I did. But I didn't mean any harm. I thought it would be okay. I didn't think she'd need her powers."

The sorrowful fuzz around Genevieve's brain thinned. *Power depressant,* echoed through her mind. How many spells had she attempted with no results? One spell, that's all it would have taken to save Hunter. One spell, and the night would have ended differently.

She squeezed her eyelids closed, wave after wave of fury hammering through her, each more intense than the last. "He's dead because I couldn't help him. He's dead because I couldn't use my magic."

Her younger sister's cheeks bloomed bright with shame,

then drained of color with regret. "I didn't think you'd need them. I didn't even think you'd notice." She clutched Genevieve's hand. "I'm so, so sorry. You have to believe I'm sorry. But think. Hunter wanted you. Not because of a potion, but because of *you*."

Genevieve's fury fizzled, leaving only despair; her muscles released their viselike grip on her bones and she sank deep into the mattress. Hunter had wanted her. Truly wanted her, without the aid of a love potion. All the things he'd said to her had come from *him*.

That made the pain of his death all the harder to bear.

I killed him. I killed him! If she hadn't decided to make Hunter love her, no matter the methods used, if she hadn't made a wish for excitement, he would still be alive. *My fault. All my fault.* Hot tears slid down her cheeks.

"Please. Leave me alone for a little while. Just leave me alone."

HUNTER'S funeral had begun an hour ago.

The digital clock blurred as Genevieve's eyes filled with tears. Any moment now, they would lower his casket into the ground and the cycle of his life—and death—would be complete.

Sobbing, she turned away from the glowing red numbers and mashed her face into her pillow. She'd never been so miserable. Her sisters had gone to the funeral. Genevieve simply wasn't ready to say good-bye.

She cried until her ducts could no longer produce tears. She cried until her throat burned and her lungs ached. Then she remained utterly still, absorbing the silence, lost in her sorrow. Minutes later, or perhaps an eternity, a buzzing sound reverberated in her left ear, and a fly landed on her cheek. Weakly she swatted the insect away.

"Bitch," she heard.

"Murderess."

"I wish *you* would have died instead."

Genevieve rolled to her back and blinked open her tired, swollen eyes. Three tiny fairies swarmed around her face, flashing pink. All three were female and scowling. She recognized them from the bar.

"You killed him," one of them hissed.

"You killed him," the others reiterated. "You could have used your magic against the demons, but you didn't. You killed him."

You killed him. Yes, she had. "I loved him." She'd thought her ducts dry, but stinging tears beaded in her eyes.

"How could you love him? You don't care about him. The demons have sworn their vengeance upon him for killing their brethren and are even now desecrating his grave, yet here you lie, doing nothing. Again. Someone even took his body from its casket."

"What?" She jolted upright. A wave of dizziness assaulted

her, and she rubbed her temple with her fingers. "Desecrating his grave, how? And who dared take his body?"

"Does it matter?" *Buzz. Buzz.* "Your sisters are fighting the demons off, but they cannot do it without you, the witch of vengeance."

Without another word, Genevieve leaped out of bed. Her knees wobbled, but a rush of adrenaline gave her strength. Arms shaking, she tugged on the first pants and T-shirt she could find, then raced through the hallway. The wolf—what had Godiva named him?—trotted to her, following close to her heels. He was almost completely healed, and his brown eyes gleamed bright with curiosity.

"There's trouble at the cemetery," she felt compelled to explain. Trouble she would fight against. Heart racing, she grabbed her broom and sprinted outside. No one—no one!—was going to destroy Hunter's grave. Whoever had taken him *would* return him.

Moonlight crested high in the night sky, scooping low. The citizens of Mysteria did everything at night, even funerals. A cool breeze ruffled her hair and kissed her fiery hot, tear-stained face. Moving faster than she ever had in her life, she hopped on her broom and flew toward Mysteria's graveyard. When she passed the wishing well, she flipped it off. When she passed Knight Caps, closed for the first time in years, she pressed her lips together to silence a pained moan.

Soon the graveyard came into view.

Monuments rose from the ground, white slashes against black dirt. Only a few patches of grass dared grow and the only flowers were silk and plastic. Death reigned supreme here. Broken brick surrounded the area with a high, eerie wall. The closer she came, the more chilled the air became, heavier, laden with the scents of dirt and mystery.

Her eyes narrowed when she saw the open, empty casket. Her eyes narrowed further when she saw the group of demons taunting her sisters and spitting on Hunter's grave.

Hunter's mourners must have already escaped, for there was no trace of them. Her sisters were holding hands and pointing their fingers toward the short, monkeylike horde of demons whose wings flapped and fluttered with excitement as they tried to claw their way through an invisible shield.

Both Godiva and Glory appeared weakened and pale, their shoulders slumped. Genevieve dropped to the ground, tossing her broom aside as she ran to them. She grabbed both of their hands, completing the link. Power instantly sparked from their fingertips. In pain, the demons shrieked.

"Thank goodness," Glory breathed. Her hands shook, but color was slowly returning to her cheeks. "I wasn't sure how much longer we could hold them off."

"There weren't this many left at the bar." Right now Genevieve counted eight. "Hunter and Falon killed a lot of them."

"They keep multiplying," Glory said. "I have a feeling

we can kill these, too, but more will come. You're the vengeance witch, Evie. Do something."

Genevieve focused all of her rage, all of her sorrow into her hands. They burned white-hot. Blistering. Her eyes slitted on her targets. "Burn," she said. "Burn."

One of the demons erupted into flames, its tortured howl echoing through the twilight. Another quickly followed. Then another and another turned to ashes, until only one remained. "Go back to hell and tell the others if they ever return I'll make their deaths a thousand times worse."

The creature vanished in a panicked puff of black smoke.

So easy. So quick. Exactly what should have happened at the bar.

Finished, depleted, she allowed her hands to fall to her sides. Weakness assaulted her as it always did when she used her powers to such a degree. She should have felt a measure of satisfaction. She should have felt vindicated. She didn't. Inside, sorrow still consumed her.

"Everyone must have raced home," Godiva panted. She hunched over, anchoring her hands on her knees. "We need to do something to prevent more demons from attacking."

"Like what?" Glory settled on the ground, her hand over her heart. "Genevieve warned them. What more can we do?"

Genevieve stared up at the stars. "A part of me wants them to return." Her tone lacked emotion, but the cold rage was there, buried under the surface. "I want to kill more of them."

Arms folded around her, comforting arms, familiar arms. "That puts other citizens at risk," Godiva said softly. "If Hunter were still alive, you'd want him protected. Let's give everyone else the same consideration."

She closed her eyes at the pain those words brought—if Hunter were alive—but nodded. Always the voice of reason, Godiva was right. If Hunter were alive, she would do whatever was necessary to protect him. "Do you know who took his body?" She gulped, the words foul on her tongue.

"No." Glory.

"No." Godiva.

Genevieve fell to her knees in front of the empty casket. Tears once more burned her eyes. There was a fresh mound of soil beside her, the spot Hunter was supposed to rest in for all of eternity, a gift to Mother Earth.

He's lost to me. No, no. She could not accept that. *Would* not accept that. "I want to raise the spirits of the dead to protect Mysteria," she found herself saying. No matter where Hunter's body was, his spirit would be able to find her—*if* she raised it. In that moment, she would have sold her soul if it meant seeing him one last time. "They can guard the town against the demons."

Pause. Silence. Not even insects dared speak.

"I don't know," Glory hedged. "Spirits are so unpredictable."

"Genevieve . . . ," Godiva began.

"Please. Do this. For me."

Her sisters glanced at each other, then at her, each other, then her. Concern darkened both of their expressions. Finally Godiva nodded. “Alright. We’ll raise the spirits, but only until the next full moon.”

Elation bubbled inside her, not obliterating her sadness but eclipsing it. *Hunter*, her heart cried again. *We’ll be together again soon. If only for a little while.*

Five

LET'S begin the spirit-raising spell." Godiva removed the band from her hair, letting the long pale strands cascade down her back. She breathed deeply of the night air. "We need to be naked for this one, so no part of our magic is trapped in the clothing fibers."

"Oh, great," was Glory's reply. She remained still, *not* stripping. "This is the twenty-first century. Do we still need to strip?"

"Yes. Now hurry and take off your clothes. I need to get home and feed Romeo." Romeo, the perfect name for her injured wolf. He'd charmed her with only a look.

Already Godiva missed him. He'd become her constant companion, a comfort in these last dark days. She wished there were something she could do for Genevieve, anything to remove the haunted glaze from her sister's eyes.

Remaining silent, Genevieve removed her clothing. Godiva unbuttoned her dress and shimmied it down her voluptuous hips. The buttercup yellow material pooled at her feet. A chill night breeze wisped around them, and with a sigh, Glory, too, stripped.

"There," she said. "Now we can begin. Form a circle and clasp hands."

The tortured howl of a wolf cut through the darkness. Godiva stilled. Had Romeo somehow gotten out of the house and now stalked the woods, searching for her? Another howl erupted through the night.

"Oh, goodness." Losing all trace of color, Glory shoved her hair out of her face. "The wolves are out. Maybe we should go home."

"We'll be fine," Godiva said, though she was worried. For a different reason. She didn't fear the wolves; she feared for Romeo. What if he got in another fight and was injured again? He might not survive this time. Her need to hurry increased.

She was just about to grab her sisters' hands when, a few feet away, her gaze snagged a silver phone and a masculine arm. Her mouth fell open. A cold sweat broke over her skin. "Girls," she whispered frantically. "Someone is taking pictures of us."

"Did you say someone is taking pictures of us?" Glory's

silver eyes narrowed. "Nobody takes secret pictures of me unless I've had time to diet."

"Don't worry. I'll handle this." Cold and emotionless, Genevieve raised her hands into the air, a dark spell slipping easily from her lips.

A startled scream echoed through the night.

"What did you do?" Glory bent down and swiped up her broom.

"See for yourself."

The girls closed ranks on the tombstone, circling the intruder and blocking him from escape. They found the flip phone hovering in the air in front of a trembling, horrified man, the phone clamping and snapping its way down his body. Only after it had bitten his favorite appendage (twice) and he screamed like a little girl (twice) did it fall to the ground.

"John Foster," Glory gasped. "You big pervert. Does Hilde know you're out here? And staring at our breasts, no less?"

"Please don't tell her—your breasts are so big." Eyes widening, he said, "I mean, I don't want her to know—I want to touch your breasts." He shook his head, but his gaze remained glued on Glory's chest. He licked his lips. "What I mean to say is—double-D fun bags are my favorite."

Glory smacked him over the head with her broom. "Letch!"

"Bastard!" Godiva grabbed her own broom and popped him dead center in the face.

"This was the wrong day to piss me off, John." Genevieve didn't have her broom in hand, so she raised her arms high in the air and uttered another incantation. "You like breasts so much, you can have a pair of your own."

His shirt ripped down the middle as a huge pair of breasts grew on his chest. He stared down at them, his mouth gaping open. "What the hell! Get them off, get them—hey, these are nice." Closing his eyes, he reached up and kneaded his new breasts, a rapturous smile spreading across his face. "Mmm," he muttered.

"Undo the spell!" Glory scowled. "Undo the spell right now. We'll punish him another way."

"No, this is punishment," he cried, covering the man-boobs protectively. "I swear. Don't take them away. I've got to learn my lesson."

Genevieve did as Glory suggested, and John's chest shrunk back to its normal size. He bawled like a baby the entire time. He even tried to dart out of their circle, but Godiva locked his feet in place with a wave of her hand.

"Not so fast," she said.

His eyes widened with horror. "What are you going to do to me? I didn't mean any harm. I only wanted a peek at your boobies."

Without saying a word, the three sisters tugged at the

rest of his clothing, peeling it from his middle-aged body until he wore nothing but a few teardrops. Since he'd gotten a look at their goods, it was only fair they got a look at his.

"Ew, gross," Glory said. "Maybe we should dress him again. I'm throwing up in my mouth."

"That will just waste more time," Godiva replied. "We're going to cast our spells around you."

Glory's gaze darted between his legs. "Yes, *little* John, we're going to cast our spells around you and you're going to stand there like a good boy or else."

That dried his tears. "You mean you're not going to hurt me, and I get to watch you dance? Naked?" He tried real hard not to grin. "How can I care about anything else when I see lots and lots of breasts and even more breasts?"

"I swear," Genevieve said, "you're the scum of the earth."

"Ignore him," Godiva said after another wolf howl echoed through the night. "We need to get to work."

"Fine."

"Yes. Let's hurry." Genevieve found her broom half buried in a mound of dirt, snatched it up, and rejoined the circle.

The three sisters closed their eyes, blocking out John's image and his voice, and in perfect sync began their protection spells. Round and round they danced, their hips undulating, their hair swaying, their brooms raised high in the air. Each one chanted under her breath.

While she danced, Godiva stumbled over the spell's

words, unable to push Romeo from her mind. That last howl had sounded pained. Was he hurt again? Should she go looking for him? He was one of the biggest, strongest, fiercest wolves she'd ever seen, but he possessed a gentle and loving nature and other beasts of the forest might trample him.

Suddenly Glory stopped, her breasts jiggling with the abrupt halt.

"What are you doing? Keep moving," John whined. "I'm still praying."

She frowned. "Does it feel like the ground is shaking?"

Godiva stilled, followed quickly by Genevieve. In the next instant and seemingly without provocation, Glory stumbled backward and landed on her butt.

"What's going on?" Godiva gasped as dirt began cracking at her feet. Grass began splitting. Flowers tumbled off of tombstones . . . and then the tombstones themselves tumbled to the ground. "What's going on?" she asked again, her tone more frenzied.

Glory popped to her feet, and Genevieve paled. "I think—ohmygoodness—I think the bodies are rising!"

"That can't be." Glory sucked in a breath, whirling around to scan the surrounding area. "We only called forth their spirits."

"Well, the dirty bastards didn't listen!"

"I don't understand. Did we say the wrong words?" Godiva asked.

A bony hand shot through the cracked dirt and latched

onto John's ankle. Startled, he screamed and would have dropped into a fetal ball and sucked his thumb if his feet hadn't been frozen in place. All over the cemetery, bodies rose. Most were completely decayed, but all still wore their worm-eaten burial clothes. As they emerged, they limped, lumbered, and trudged toward the sisters. Deadly moans echoed across the distance.

"What should we do?" Glory gasped out, holding out her broom like a sword. "What the hell should we do?"

Agnes McCloud—a woman everyone knew had once been John's mistress—climbed all the way out of the ground. Seeing her, John started shaking like an epileptic. "Help me," he cried. "Please, help me. Free my feet."

Godiva swatted at the skeleton with her broom. "Shoo." Big chunks of dirt fell out of the dead woman's hair. "Get back in the ground. I command you."

Agnes was only recently dead from a car accident, and her face lifted into a grin when she spied John. "John! Oh, my darling Johnnie. I missed you so much."

"We've got to send them back." Glory's mouth formed a large O as she counted the number of bodies headed toward them. "They're multiplying like rabbits!"

"Demons of the Dark," Godiva shouted, "return to your graves!"

They kept coming.

"Spirits of the Netherworld, be gone!"

Still, they kept coming.

Meanwhile, Agnes had pounced on John and was feasting on him like he was a buffet of sensual delights and she had been on a year-long fast. Except, the man looked like he would rather eat his own vomit than the dead woman's tongue. That didn't stop Agnes.

If she'd had time, Godiva would have snapped a picture of the two with the flip phone. As it was, the rest of the dead bodies finally reached them and closed her and her sisters in a circle, moaning and groaning and reaching out to caress them. Having been without human contact for so long, they were probably desperate for it. Or maybe they were simply hungry and she and her sisters looked like a triple-stacked Egg McMuffin.

Glory shrieked. Godiva swatted at the bony hands with her broom. And Genevieve stood in frozen shock. "Is that . . . Hunter?"

A male form broke through the line of trees, just beyond the cemetery. His skin was intact, his features normal. Except for his eyes. They glowed a bright, vivid red. Obviously, he wasn't a corpse. But . . . what was he?

"Hunter!" Genevieve called excitedly. "Ohmygoodness, Hunter, over here!"

He turned toward the sound of her voice, and his lips lifted in relief. "Genevieve!"

They sprinted to each other, avoiding dead bodies and Genevieve threw herself into his arms. Godiva couldn't hear what they were saying. She watched as Hunter flung Genevieve over his shoulder and carted her straight into the forest.

"Godiiiiiva," Glory gasped. "Don't just stand there. Help me!"

She shook her head and continued to fight off their molesters with her broom, all the while uttering spell after ineffectual spell. Well, not so ineffectual. Each spell conjured something—just not the help they wanted. A fairy. A gnome. A gorgeous demon high lord. Why were their spells messing up? She still didn't understand. Each creature materialized at the edge of the forest and stood, watching the proceedings, grinning. One of them even produced a bowl of popcorn and a large soda.

"Two dollars says the one with worms in his eyes snags the witch on the left," the demon said.

"You're on," the gnome agreed.

Suddenly a fierce growl overshadowed every other noise, and a pack of wolves raced into the graveyard, snapping and snarling.

"Romeo," Godiva cried, her relief nearly a palpable force when she recognized her pet.

His teeth bared in a menacing scowl, Romeo leaped up and latched onto the bony arm reaching for her and snapped it off before sprinting away.

"Give that back," the corpse shouted, chasing after him.

The rest of the wolf pack chased the skeletons in every

direction. All except Agnes, who was still sucking John's face. Godiva and Glory dropped to the ground in relief.

"I never thought I'd be grateful to the wolves," Glory said. "Should we be worried for Genevieve?"

"No. I think she'll be fine." More than fine, actually. "Here, take my hand. We have to send these corpses back to their graves."

Glory intertwined their fingers. Without the fear of being eaten, they were able to concentrate on their spell. As they chanted, magic began to swirl around them, drifting through the cemetery and luring each dead body back to its grave.

Suddenly, Falon—who had not come to Hunter's funeral, for some reason—burst from the forest and came running toward them. Rage consumed his features. Godiva blinked over at him in surprise—she'd never seen him move so quickly or so lethally—and from the corner of her eye she saw Glory jolt up, panic storming over her expression.

"I'm naked," Glory said, her voice frantic. "Where are my clothes? Falon can't see me naked!" Her movements jerky, she searched the dirt, found the yellow dress Godiva had worn, and tugged it over her head.

Falon skidded to an abrupt stop in front of Glory. "Are you alright?"

His gaze focused on Glory, and Godiva was amused to realize she herself could have been a bloody, writhing mass and he wouldn't have noticed. Still, she scrambled for the clothing littering the ground, a pair of stone-washed jeans and a pink sweater.

"We're fine," Glory said stiffly. She pushed to her feet and smoothed her hair out of her face, looking anywhere but at Falon. "How did you know we were in trouble?"

A tinge of color darkened his cheeks. "I sensed it."

Well, well, well. Godiva had never seen the two exchange a single word, yet here they were, acting as if they knew each other. How interesting. Sexual attraction sparked between them, white-hot, intense. Nearly palpable.

"Well, you're too late," Glory told Falon. "We took care of everything ourselves."

Just then Romeo appeared in front of Godiva, claiming her attention. "There's my good boy," she said, reaching out for him. He dropped an arm bone at her feet as if it were the greatest prize in the world and nuzzled her with his nose. She luxuriated in his soft black fur as his tongue flicked out and licked her collarbone. "I'm glad you're okay."

"Eww." Glory balled her fists on her hips. "I know I've said your boyfriends were dogs in the past, but hello. This one *is* a dog. Don't let him lick you like that. Have him neutered, at the very least."

"He's my special sweetie." She rubbed her cheek against his. "My hero."

Glory turned on her heel. "I'm outta here," she called over her shoulder.

"I'll walk you home," Falon said.

She didn't bother glancing in his direction. "No, you won't."

"I wasn't asking. I was telling." The determined man strode to Glory's side, keeping pace beside her.

"I don't need your help, jerk-off."

"I'm giving it anyway."

Their voices faded. Romeo growled at Glory's retreating back, then looked up into the sky and howled. As he howled, his body elongated and his fur fell away. Godiva gasped and jerked away from him. Skin and muscled ridges were forming. Ribs, fingers, and toes. Bronzed skin.

"Romeo?" she asked, frightened. Her mouth went dry, and her heart pounded against her ribs. He was . . . beautiful. "Romeo?" The name emerged on a breathless catch of air this time.

Dark gold *human* eyes were suddenly staring down at her, and she drank in the most beautiful face she'd ever seen. Perfectly chiseled cheekbones, perfectly sloped nose. Full, lush pink lips made for kissing. Her gaze traveled downward, taking in the rest of him. His chest was wide and muscled, like velvet poured over steel. And his— "Sweet mercy."

"I've been dying to do this all week, but was afraid you'd stop coddling and petting me." He grinned wickedly. "You are not mad?"

His voice was rough and husky, and so sexy she shivered. Gulping, she blinked up at him. “Not mad. Promise.”

“I would like a chance to coddle *you*. Let me take you home.”

To bed, echoed in her mind, unsaid. “Yes. Take me home.”

Six

"YOU'RE here," Genevieve said as Hunter slid her down his body. "You're really here." She circled him, disbelief, joy, and sexual hunger eating at her. Pink pollen twirled around them.

Hunter remained utterly still. He was as harshly gorgeous as ever, only somehow more savage looking. Her heart thrummed with excitement, even as confusion rocked her. "How are you here? You aren't a corpse and you aren't a spirit, but you've been gone for three days."

Trees swayed around them, and the scent of moon-magic and jasmine wafted headily through the air. Rays of muted light illuminated the clearing.

"I . . . didn't die," he said. He stared at her neck, his eyes red. "I should leave."

"No! Stay." She bit her bottom lip. Never had she been more overjoyed, more confused. "Why are your eyes red? Wait, the red is fading. I don't understand. What happened to you?"

He didn't answer.

She forgot the question, anyway, as she reached out, hands brushing his jacket to the ground. *She* was already naked; she wanted *him* naked, too. Nothing else mattered really. Next she unbuttoned his shirt. It, too, pooled at their feet. Her fingers met his chest, paler than before but strong.

"I missed you so much," she told him. "When I thought you were dead, I wanted to die, too."

"Genevieve," he said, the sound of her name a moan of pleasure-pain. He squeezed his eyelids together. "I should go. You're safe now."

"Don't leave. Stay with me. Please."

"Something happened—"

"However you survived, I don't care. I just want you." She flattened her palms over his chest, his nipples deliciously abrasive. "Mmm. So good."

His hands tangled in her hair, and their gazes locked. "I want to kiss you."

"Do it. Kiss me."

He leaned toward her and nuzzled his nose over her neck. "You smell so good. Better than I remembered." The more he spoke, the more slurred his words became.

"Kiss me, Hunter. Please."

He paused only a moment before straightening and crushing his lips against hers. His tongue slid into her mouth, already heating, already slick and flavored with passion. He tasted like urgency. They'd been apart so long—days that seemed to have stretched beyond eternity.

Her hands tore at the button on his pants, and in seconds, he was naked. All the while, he rained little kisses over her entire face. Desire rushed through her blood. "No more waiting," she said breathlessly.

"No more waiting," he agreed. Something dark blanketed his expression, his eyes suddenly going red again. "I'm not going to hurt you," he said, his voice rough, filled with determination.

"I know."

"Good." He tumbled her to the ground. His lips clamped around her hard, aching nipple, and his hand trailed down her stomach, raising gooseflesh. He stopped at the apex of her thighs, dabbling at the fine tuft of dark hair.

"Yes, good," she moaned.

She kneaded her hands down his strong torso, reveling in the hard muscles hidden under male skin. Power radiated from him. *My lover,* she thought dazedly. *My man. Mine, all mine.* The passion, the desire, the pleasure he gave her surpassed her wildest imaginings. And he hadn't even entered her yet.

He began sucking her nipple, his teeth surprisingly sharp, wringing another gasp from her. He licked away the delicious sting. "I'm not going to hurt you, I'm not going to hurt you, I'm not going to hurt you," he chanted.

"You can't. As long as you're with me, you can't."

"How did I push you away all these years?" His voice was strained, laden with carnal intent, heavy with arousal.

She arched into his fingers, silently begging him to move them inside her. No, wait. She stilled. Before she forgot everything but his touch, she wanted to fulfill the fantasy that had been floating through her mind for years. "I want to take you in my mouth."

Like a sea siren of long ago, she rose over him, her hair falling like a dark curtain. She walked her fingers down the muscled ridge of his chest. Scars slashed left and right over his ribs, jagged badges of past pain. This was not the body of a bar owner. This was the body of a warrior.

He sucked in a breath when she licked each of his nipples. He moaned when she cupped his testicles.

"You aren't just a bar owner," she said, voicing her thoughts and blowing a hot puff of air on his abdomen. His muscles quivered. "You're much more."

"Yes, but I don't want to talk about it. Move a little lower, sweetheart, and help me forget." He growled, and hearing that desire-rough growl made her shiver.

"Besides running the bar, what is it you do?" she persisted. She wanted to know him. She didn't want to simply be his lover, she wanted to be his confidante. His . . . everything.

A muscle ticked in his jaw. "Hunt vampires, demons, and other creatures of the night. That's how I got my name."

She circled his navel with her tongue. His hips shot toward the sky.

"Have you destroyed very many?" she asked.

"Many." An aroused breath shuddered past his lips, and his eyes closed. "Then I met you and decided to settle here and now I think it'd be a really good idea if you moved a little lower. I don't want to talk about the past anymore."

Shock brought her to an instant halt. "You settled here because of me?"

"Yes."

Surprised, happy, she sucked the entire length of his penis into her mouth. He was so big, her mouth stretched wide.

He began to babble. "I was afraid another gnome would try and hurt you, couldn't let that happen, had to stay near you, damn you feel so good, I need to get inside you. Oh, that feels good. Your mouth. Heaven."

"I love you," she said, never ceasing her up and down strokes.

His hips shot up, and he growled low in his throat. Hoarse. Animalistic. She worked him, savoring every sensation, every taste.

"Holy hell, I can't stop," he managed to gasp.

She sucked him dry.

When he lay limp, collapsed against the dried leaves and

twigs, she crawled over him. Feminine power filled her, and she grinned slowly, wickedly. "I've wanted to do that for a long time."

"Not nearly as much as I wanted you to do it." Twin circles of pink painted his cheeks. "I didn't mean to go off so quickly. That just felt so good, and it's been so long, and it made me forget—" He cut himself off and pressed his lips in a thin line.

"How long has it been?" The question sprung from her before she could stop it. She didn't want to hear about his other women. Wanted him only to think of her. Her body, her mind. Her heart.

"About a year," he admitted sheepishly.

He pushed her to her back with quite a bit of force, and she smashed into the ground with a gasp.

Instantly he frowned. "I'm sorry, baby. I didn't mean to push so hard."

"Don't be sorry. I'm not hurt." Smiling seductively, she stretched her arms toward him. "I like it when you're rough."

His expression softened, and his gaze raked over her. Desire blazed all the hotter in the blue depths of his eyes. No longer red, she realized happily. Why did they turn red? Was he a demon now? If so, she didn't care. He bent between her legs, his warm breath fanning the very heart of her. Her mind blanked. Already she trembled for the first stroke of his tongue, for the ache she'd always dreamed about, for the completion she'd always wanted. Needed.

He tasted her. His tongue circled her clitoris, an erotic dance that spun her through madness, through heaven. "Hunter," she cried, arching against him.

"That's it, baby." His voice was strained. "Go all the way over the edge."

Her legs wrapped around his neck, locking him in place. The pressure . . . the building . . . an unstoppable crescendo. When he brought his fingers into play, sinking them deep inside her, she realized the pleasure had only just begun.

"I won't hurt you, I won't hurt you, I won't hurt you." His voice vibrated through her. "You taste so good."

She continued to arch, writhing, screaming her pleasure to the twinkling stars. Her magic acted as a live wire, shooting fireworks in her blood. Then, everything crested. High, so high. Her inner walls spasmed; heat exploded inside her. So much sensation, more than she could bear, yet not enough and somehow everything.

She must have squeezed her eyelids tightly shut because Hunter was suddenly hovering over her. His eyes were red again, and sweat trickled down his temples. Lines of tension bracketed that sweet mouth of his, as if he'd endured all he could and needed satisfaction.

"I'm going to enter you now, but I won't hurt you. I'm going to fill you with me, but I won't hurt you."

"Yes. Please, yes!"

"I won't hurt you." Slowly he slid inside her, his cock stretching her, filling her as he'd promised. He moaned. She gasped. Tension tightened his features. "You're so tight. I didn't expect you to be this tight."

"More. I need more. Do it, take me the rest of the way."

He required no further encouragement. He pushed the rest of the way home. Her legs tightened around him. Squeezed his waist. Her virginity tore. Destroyed perfectly. Wonderfully.

"Virgin," he said, shocked. His eyes closed. Pleasure blanketed his expression. "Never felt this . . . good. This right. I can smell the blood. So good." He licked his lips as if he'd never experienced anything so delicious and wanted to savor the sensation. "So good."

"Only you would . . . do. Harder," she rasped.

"No, savor," he intoned. "I won't hurt you. Won't . . . hurt . . . you."

Her hands gripped his butt at the same moment she rocked her hips upward, "Savor," she allowed, barely able to get the word out. She wanted him inside her forever.

His teeth bit into his bottom lip. "No, harder."

"Yes, yes. Harder."

He slammed inside, pulled back, and pounded home.

"Yes!" she shouted, loving the feel of his in-and-out penetration.

"Not. Hurt. Not. Hurt." He moved so quickly his balls slapped her. She threaded her fingers in his hair and jerked his face to her. Her tongue thrust into his mouth. Taking. Giving. Pushing her even closer to the edge.

"You can't hurt me, I swear."

He reached between their bodies, rubbed his thumb over her clitoris, and that was it. The end. She erupted. Spasmed. Arched. Screamed. Her ecstasy vibrated into his body, propelling him to the end, as well.

"Genevieve," he howled. His features tightened further and he pounded into her a final time.

Minutes passed, perhaps hours, before their breathing settled. His eyes were so red they lit up the entire forest, and he was staring at her neck. He licked his lips. She didn't move. Couldn't, for that matter. Satisfaction thrummed and swirled inside her, the madness gone, delicious lethargy in its place. "I love you," she said.

Hunter suddenly jerked from her as if she were poison. "I have to leave, Genevieve. I'm sorry." His expression was tortured. "I'm beginning to lose control. Barnabas was right. When the hunger hit . . ." He spun away from her.

"What—what are you talking about?"

"Good-bye. I'll never forget you." He jolted into a lightning-fast run, never once looking back.

Seven

IF not for her witchy powers, Genevieve never would have caught him. He moved unbelievably fast. As it was, she uttered a transport spell under her breath. One moment she was lying on the forest floor, the next she was standing in front of Hunter.

He snarled in his throat and ground to a halt. "Get away from me!"

"Tell me what's going on," she commanded. Moonlight shimmered between them, painting the forest in a magical golden hue. "Are you part demon?"

Hunter shoved a hand through his hair and turned away from her—exactly like he'd done in the past. "I lied to you earlier, Genevieve. I *did* die. After the fight with the demons, Barnabas Vlad took my body to an underground cave. He—

he turned me into a vampire." His voice was laced with pain and sounded . . . tortured.

Ah. Now she understood the red eyes. She owed Barnabas a smorgasbord of human delights dinner, no doubt about it. "This is a good thing, Hunter. We can be together now."

Gaze rounding, he whirled on her. "I'm a monster. I want to drink your blood."

"Well, I'm a witch and you accepted me for who I am."

"Stop. Just stop. It's not the same. I could kill you, but your powers can't harm me."

"Yes, they can." Determined, she raised her arms in the air and summoned forth a small beam of light. Not enough to burn him, just enough to prove her point. Golden rays began to ribbon from her fingertips.

He raised his hands to shield his eyes. "Fine. Your powers can destroy me. You, at least, can control them."

She dropped her arms to her sides and the light dimmed completely.

"Even now I'm close to jumping on you and sinking my teeth into your neck, Genevieve. I'm thirsty, and I can smell the sweetness of your blood. I'm vile and disgusting and *terrible*."

"Hunter," she said, exasperated. She threw her arms in the air. Men—correction, vampires—could be so foolish. "If you want to drink from me, I don't mind." She flicked back her hair, revealing the sensuous line of her neck. "I promise."

"Argh." He spun away quickly, his body stiff, his hands clenched. "Don't do that again."

"Or what?"

"You don't know vampires like I do. Once they get a drop of blood in their mouth, they can't stop. I could take too much. I could kill you."

"You won't hurt me," she said in utter confidence. "You said so yourself, a thousand times. Bite me. Do it. Blood, blood, blood. I'll keep saying it until you get over here and bite me. Blood, blood, bl—"

Hunter pivoted on his heel and closed the distance between them. He captured her face with his hands, his eyes fierce, but he didn't bite her. He bared his teeth, sharp and white, but still he didn't bite her. "Shut. Up. I would rather live eternity without you than to know I drained you."

She saw the depth of his concern for her, and desperation churned inside her. If she didn't show him the error of his thoughts, he was going to leave her. Forever. "If you walk away from me, you're going to hurt me."

A pause.

A heavy, sickening pause.

"Genevieve." His fingers traced her mouth, then dipped to her neck. He fingered the pulse hammering there. "I won't allow myself to become a killer."

She wrapped her arms around his waist, locking him in place. "I barely survived our first parting. How am I going to live without you?" The idea alone filled her eyes with tears. After all the years she and Hunter had been apart, they deserved a happy-ever-after.

"You'll live. That's all that matters." He spanned his hands around her waist, holding her with such fervency she had trouble drawing in a breath, but she didn't care. What was breath without Hunter's scent? What was life without her reason for living?

"Bite me," she commanded him. As she spoke, she arched her head to the side. She *had* to prove to him that he wouldn't kill her. "Blood, blood, blood, bloo—"

With a pained growl, he swooped down as if he'd reached the edge of his tolerance and sank his sharp teeth into her vein. There was a stinging prick, and she gasped. A minute passed, then another, but he didn't stop. The sensations began to feel good, so good. He drank and drank and drank, and her mind began to grow foggy. Her limbs became weak. Black wisps twined around her thoughts.

"Hunter," she gasped. "I'm . . ."

He jerked from her as if she'd screamed. She slumped to the ground. Panting, he stood over her body. Blood dripped from his mouth and guilt filled his eyes. "I'm sorry. Sweet heaven, I'm sorry."

"I'm fine, I'm fine." She was panting. "I swear. You stopped in time."

"No. Too close. In the morning, I'm going to walk into the sun," he said, his voice so ragged with determination it emerged as nothing more than a feral snarl. “There’s no other way. I’ll keep coming for you otherwise, I know I will.”

In the next instant, he was gone.

“Hunter. Hunter!” Weak, she lumbered to her feet. She screeched a transport spell, but it didn’t work. Her magic had weakened with her body.

Genevieve scanned the forest. Where was he? Where had he gone? *I’m going to walk into the sun*, he’d said. “I’m okay. I survived. You didn’t hurt me, only weakened me a bit.” Not allowing herself to panic—yet—she stumbled through the trees. “Hunter, please!”

Branches swayed on a gentle cascade of wind. Birds scattered, soaring into the night sky, their wings striped with every color of the rainbow. If morning came before she found him . . .

“Hunter! Hunter!” She twirled as she shouted, still searching. Minutes passed. Horrendous, agonizing minutes.

He never reappeared.

HUNTER made it to the caves in seconds. He’d moved so quickly that the world around him became a blur, that the five miles seemed like less than one.

Barnabas was still there, still sitting on the dais. The cave walls were rocky and bare. Bleak. Like his emotions. Hunter didn’t know why he’d come here. Here, of all places. With *this* man. He simply hadn’t known where else to go. He’d bitten Genevieve and had almost drained her. If she hadn't uttered his name . . . Shame coursed through him.

"Couldn't stay away, I see," Barnabas said smugly.

Dejected, Hunter wiped the sweet, magical blood from his mouth. "I'm walking into the sun, vampire. I'm too wretched to live."

"I told you the hunger would hit you, and you wouldn't be able to control it." Barnabas used his too sharp teeth to tug off one of his black gloves. "You should have listened to me, *oui?*" He *tsked*. "Now. Would you like to play a game of strip poker? I brought cards."

"No cards." Hunter could still smell Genevieve on him, could still taste her mystical-flavored blood in his mouth. His hands clenched at his sides, and he found himself stepping toward the entrance, ready to go to her again. "Damn it." He froze. "Morning can't get here fast enough."

Barnabas sighed, and the sound dripped with dejection. "I'm going to lose you one way or the other, aren't I? Through death or through your woman, and I think I would rather it be your woman."

Hunter's eyes narrowed. "What are you talking about?"

"Sit down, and I will tell you a secret. . . ."

AT last giving way to her panic, Genevieve raced into the thankfully empty cemetery and gathered her clothes. Her neck ached; she didn't care. Her fingers shaky, she tugged on the pants, the shirt. All of the gravesites were in complete disarray, dirt crumbled, headstones overturned. Where was Hunter? She had to find him before it was too late. Her fear intensified, joining ranks with her panic. Her gaze scanned the area until she found her broom. She hopped on it and commanded it to fly.

It didn't work. Fine.

Holding on to it, she ran, just ran. By the time she reached the center of town, her lungs burned and her heart raced uncontrollably. People were in their yards and on the streets, cleaning up damage the demons had caused. No one paid her any heed.

She spotted John Foster hiding behind a tree in his front yard, watching the lusciously ripe Candy Cox rake her garden. "Have any of you seen Hunter Knight?" Genevieve called.

John squealed in horror and sprinted away.

"No, sorry," Candy replied with a frown. "Hunter's dead, sugar. I doubt I'll be seeing him for a while."

Panting, Genevieve ran to Knight Caps. She searched every room, every hidden corridor, but the place was empty. Nothing had been cleaned; everything was the same as on the night Hunter died. Overturned tables, liquor spilled on the floor. Pools of dried blood.

She sprinted back outside and down the long, winding

streets. Finally she reached the white picket fence surrounding her home. She pounded up the porch steps and shoved past the screen door, tossing her broom aside. "Godiva! Glory!" She was so short of breath she had trouble getting the words out.

A few seconds later, Glory stumbled out of her room. She rubbed the sleep from her eyes. The buttercup yellow flannel pj's she wore hung over her curves like a sack. "What's going on?" She yawned. "Are you okay?"

"Have you seen Hunter?"

"No. I thought he was with you. What's with his red eyes, anyway? Is he a demon?"

She didn't bother with an answer. "Where's Godiva?"

"In her room. With Romeo."

"Who?"

"Romeo. Her wolf." Glory stretched her arms over her head and gave another yawn. "I think they're having sex. Again."

"Stop playing around and tell me where Godiva is. Please. I don't have much time."

"I told you. In bed. Nice hickey, by the way." Glory paused, her gaze skidding to the kitchen. "Oh, look. Doughnuts." She breezed past Genevieve and headed into the kitchen, where a box of Krispy Kremes waited on the table.

"Godiva!" Genevieve shouted. "Get out here right now."

The handle to Godiva's bedroom rattled, then the door

pushed open. Out toppled Godiva, tightening her robe around her middle. She wore an expression of concern, yet underneath the concern was utter satisfaction. "Is everything okay?"

"Have you seen Hunter?"

"No, I thought he was with you."

A warrior of a man stepped from the room and approached Godiva from behind. He wrapped his strong arms around her waist. Dark hair tumbled to his shoulders, framing a face of such golden-eyed beauty Genevieve found it difficult to believe he was real. Her mouth fell open as realization struck her. *This* was the injured wolf?

"What's going on, Evie? Is everything okay?" Godiva repeated. "Your neck is bleeding."

"Hunter is a vampire, and he plans to die with the morning sun. I have to find him. Can you transport me to him?" She covered her face with her hand, fighting tears. "I can't let him kill himself."

"You know we can't transport other people. I can transport myself, though, and—"

"You are not transporting yourself in front of a vampire, Godiva," Romeo said, his voice deep, gravelly. "We will search together. I can track humans—even dead ones—in ways you cannot."

Grateful, Genevieve nodded. She would have ridden on the broom with Godiva, but Godiva couldn't find hers. "I must have left it in the graveyard," her sister said. Genevieve still didn't have the strength to fire hers up, and Glory couldn't hold both of them. They walked.

They kept pace beside Romeo, who took wolf form. They ended up searching all night, stopping only to drink. No one had seen Hunter, and only a few people seemed surprised that they were asking about a dead guy.

Finally, only thirty minutes till sunrise, Romeo caught a trace of him. "This way."

"Hurry. Hurry." She wanted to scream in relief, in frustration, in agony. But when Romeo led them back to her house, she did scream. "Damn it! Why did you bring us here? He's—" She gasped as her gaze snagged on the man standing on her porch.

"Genevieve," he said starkly.

"Hunter? Hunter!" With a cry, she raced to him.

Eight

HUNTER opened his arms and welcomed Genevieve as she threw herself at him. He twirled her around, reveling in her luscious female scent, the soft curves of her body.

"Where have you been?" she demanded. "You stupid, stupid man. I've been so worried about you. You didn't hurt me out there, okay? You didn't hurt me. You stopped in time."

"I *could* have hurt you, and that was enough reason to die." He pulled back and cupped her face in his hands. Would he ever get enough of this woman?

Tears streamed down her face. "Why are you here, then? Why?"

"I talked to Barnabas. His creator hated and feared blood, like me, so he took something called a blood-appetite suppressant. I didn't think it'd work, but I took it and my cravings went away. I won't hurt you now. I know it sounds too good to be true," he rushed on, "but it's true. Trust me not to hurt you. Please. I want to be with you."

"Why do you want to be with me?" she interjected. In that moment, her relief and joy overflowed, but she needed to hear the words.

His expression became tender. "I kept picturing your face and I began to realize that even in death, you would haunt me. I began to realize that leaving you would be more vile than drinking from you. I began to realize that I couldn't leave you again. You're my reason for being. You're my everything."

She blinked through her tears, barely daring to breathe.

"Will you have me, Genevieve Tawdry? Vampire that I am?"

"With all of my heart." Laughing, she kissed him over and over again. Loving kisses, happy kisses. Relieved kisses.

Hunter hugged her fiercely. That laugh of hers . . . glorious, uninhibited, he would never get enough of it. "I want you. I want you naked."

"Uh, Genevieve," came a female voice.

Genevieve's cheeks reddened, and she pressed her lips together. She'd forgotten about their audience, he realized with satisfaction, just as he had.

"Hunter, you know my sisters."

He nodded in their direction, but his eyes were only for

Genevieve. "Godiva. Glory. Nice to see you again." His fingers played with the silky soft hair at the base of Genevieve's neck. He couldn't stop touching her. He still didn't like the fact that he was a vampire. He still didn't like that he had to drink blood, even though the cravings could be controlled. But he would put up with anything to be with his Genevieve.

"You, too," they said simultaneously.

"The man with Godiva is Romeo," she said breathlessly. Her eyes closed and a look of rapture blanketed her expression. "You can meet him later."

Romeo nodded in acknowledgment. He placed a protective arm around Godiva, as if Hunter might leap off the porch and attack at any moment. Hunter tried not to take offense. He had better get used to people fearing him.

"Hunter and I are going to my room," Genevieve said. "To, uh, talk."

"Dirty," Glory added.

He allowed Genevieve to take his hand and lead him inside, down a hallway and into her room. It was a neat, tidy space with everything color-coded and organized. The bed was made for sin, however. Black silks, crimson pillows. Cerulean velvets. "You want to talk?" he asked with a chuckle.

Her lips lifted in a sensual grin that caused his stomach to clench. She hurriedly secured all of the drapes over the windows so that when the sun rose, it wouldn't hurt him. "We can talk while you're inside me." She raced to him and tugged at his clothes. "I need you so desperately."

He slipped her shirt over her head, then pushed her pants to her ankles. She stepped out of them, completely naked. The sight of her naked beauty almost made him come, right then, right there. Supple curves, ripe nipples, milky skin. The long length of her dark hair provided a mesmerizing contrast.

"I can't wait," he said raggedly.

"No waiting," she agreed.

He took her quickly, with all the urgency he felt inside. Filled as he was with blood and the suppressant, he didn't have the slightest urge to bite her—except in pleasure. They rolled atop the bed, panting, growling, straining. Her breasts filled his hands. Her legs anchored around him as he pounded in and out.

"Hunter," she screamed as a sharp peak tore through her. He felt every spasm and it fueled his own.

He spilled inside her with a loud roar.

Someone banged at the wall. "Enough already," he heard one of her sisters say. Glory, most likely. Godiva was probably otherwise occupied. He chuckled into Genevieve's neck. Nope. He still didn't want to bite her. Relief consumed him.

Playfully she bit his collarbone. "I love you so much."

Her words filled his mind as surely as he'd filled her body. Even his heart stopped beating—or maybe it had never started up again after his death. Women had said those words to him before, but he'd never felt them in his bones. Even Genevieve had said them before. He'd never returned them.

"I love you, too, sweetheart."

She sucked in a slight intake of breath. "Do you really?"

"I've loved you from the first moment I saw you."

"Then why did you push me away for so long?" she asked with a frown. "You never really answered that question."

He placed a sweet kiss on her temple. "Sweetheart, the answer doesn't matter anymore. Let's just—"

"Please. Tell me."

Unable to deny her anything, he explained. As he spoke, she paled. Tremors reverberated through her by the time he finished. "You should have told me the truth years ago," she said. "I would have left you alone."

"I know, and that's exactly why I didn't tell you. I didn't want you to leave me alone. I loved you too damn much."

"What a pair we make, hmm? The dead man and the witch."

He chuckled. Life—or death, rather—was ripe with promise. He was happier than he'd ever been and he owed it all to the sweet, sweet witch in his arms. "I'm looking forward to spending eternity with you."

Slowly she smiled. "Eternity with Hunter Knight. Now that's something I can look forward to."

A Tawdry Affair

To P. C. Cast, Susan Grant, and MaryJanice Davidson.
Or, as we would probably be named inside of Mysteria:
P. C. Sweetbottoms, Susan Buttercup,
and MaryJanice Sugarlips.
(Maybe I'd be Gena Dinglehop—that's wait-and-see, though.)
To Wendy McCurdy and Allison Brandau
for putting up with me!

One

IF Glory Tawdry discovered her sister, Evie, and Evie's vampire boyfriend going at it like wild cougars one more time—just one more!—she was going to throw up a lung, gouge out her eyes, and cut off her ears.

"You're disgusting," she grumbled, standing in Evie's *open* bedroom door. Her sister and Hunter must have severe discovery fantasies, because they always "forgot" to barricade themselves inside when things were getting heated.

They didn't even glance in her direction.

She coughed.

They continued.

Sadly, if Glory walked down the hallway of their modest little three-bedroom home, she'd probably hear her other sister, Godiva, going at it with *her* boyfriend, a werewolf shape-shifter. They, at least, liked privacy when they were screaming like hyenas.

Still. There was no peace to be found for Glory. Not even in town. Lately Mysteria, a place once known for its evil creature population, as well as a place she'd taken great pride in, had turned into a horrifying love fest of goo-goo eyes and butt pinching.

Except for me. No one makes goo-goo eyes at me. No one pinches my *butt, even though there's enough for everyone to grab on to at the same time.* She didn't care, though. Really.

Men and relationships were so not for her. Really.

"Hello," she said, trying again. "I'm right here. Can you stop for like a minute?"

Thankfully Evie and Hunter finished their show and collapsed side by side under the covers. Moonlight spilled from the beveled windows and onto the bed, painting them in gold. Both were panting, sweat glistening from their skin. Evie's dark hair was spread over the pillow and tangled under Hunter's arm. Vitality radiated from her.

Handsome Hunter looked exhausted and incapable of movement.

Score one for Evie, Glory supposed.

"Oh, Glory." Evie grinned, happiness sparkling in her hazel eyes. "I didn't see you there."

Ugh. Evie did everything happily now, and Glory was seriously embarrassed for her. Evie was the greatest vengeance witch ever to live in Mysteria. As such, she should scowl once in a while. *Glory* was the love witch, damn it, so *Glory* should be the happy one.

"Don't you know how to knock?" her sister asked.

Are you freaking kidding me? "Don't you know how to close a door? I mean, it's a difficult task to master, but with hard work and the proper training, I think you might be able to do it."

Hunter laughed, revealing long, sharp teeth.

"Ha-ha." Evie punched him on the shoulder.

When Evie said no more, Glory shook her head in disappointment. Used to, they would have argued and insulted each other, maybe yelled and thrown things. Now, she was lucky if Evie frowned at her.

A dysfunctional relationship it had been, but it had been *theirs*.

"I miss us!" she found herself saying. "You're a softie now, and it's killing my excitement levels."

Understanding dawned, and Evie scowled. Even pointed an accusing finger at her. "Seriously, what's up with you, little sis? Every day I think you can't possibly get any bitchier, and then you go and prove me wrong."

Much better! Life was suddenly worth living again. "Lookit, you show pony, I need your help."

"Yeah? With what?" Unable to retain the harsh expression, Evie gave her another smile.

As always, that satisfied smile caused a deep ache to

sprout inside Glory's chest. *When will it be my turn to fall in love, have great sex, and sicken the people around me?* The moment the thought drifted through her mind, she blinked in shock and revulsion. *Whoa, girl. That line of BS has to stop. Like, now. Before you crave more.*

She was a love witch, yes, but *she* didn't want to fall in love. Ever. People became slobbering fools when they succumbed to the soft emotion. Look at Evie! Proof right there in all her glowing splendor.

"I'm waiting," Evie said.

Glory opened her mouth to say . . . something. What, she didn't know. Just how should she begin? She could *not* allow Evie to turn her down.

"Seriously. I want to bask in the afterglow." Evie rubbed her leg up and down Hunter's lower torso. "Hurry this along."

"I'm thinking."

Evie sighed. And yes, she was still smiling. "Go think somewhere else."

"You left your door open, so no afterglow for you. One year," she said in her best "Soup Nazi" impersonation. Glory tangled a hand through her hair, surprised as always that it was cool to the touch. Every time she saw the flame red tresses in the mirror, she expected smoke. *I can do this.* "Remember a few months ago, when Hunter was ignoring you—again—and you promised me a favor if I helped you win his heart? I told you that in return for helping you, I wanted you to give me something to ruin Falon's life, and you said okay, so I gave you a potion and you—"

"I know what I did. Jeez." Nibbling on her lower lip, Evie moved her hazels to Hunter.

He knew the full story, but Glory suspected Evie didn't like to remind him. He'd died because of Evie, after all, killed by demons the lovesick fool had accidentally summoned. *Then* he'd been turned into a vampire—a species he'd once hoped to destroy. It had been difficult for him to adjust to the change.

"You want to ruin Falon's life? Why?" Hunter's vampire-pale arms tightened around Evie. Obviously no bad feelings remained on his part. But he did frown over at Glory as if she had sprouted a second head. With horns. Falon was his best friend and right-hand man.

At least, Glory thought Falon was a man. In Mysteria, it was sometimes hard to tell. He could have been a demon for all she knew. Now that made sense. "Just . . . because," she said, then squared her shoulders and raised her chin. She refused to say more about her reasoning. "Evie owes me. That should be enough."

Evie threw up her arms and let them fall heavily onto the bed. "Can't you drop this? I don't know what he did to you . . ." She paused, probably waiting for Glory to pipe up with the answer. When she didn't, Evie sighed again. "You live in Bizarro World, little sis. You're supposed to be the good witch, and *I'm* supposed to be wicked."

Glory arched a brow, her mind caught on the first part of Evie's speech. "No, I can't let this go." The bastard deserved to die. Slowly. Painfully. Eternally. "You reneging on me?"

Hot color bloomed in her sister's cheeks. "No. Of course not."

"Evie," Hunter said.

"I promised her, baby."

Glory anchored her hands on her hips. "If it makes you feel any better, Hunter, know that Falon brought this on himself. He hurt me."

Hunter's green gaze sharpened. "Hurt you? How?"

Once again, she raised her chin and pressed her lips together. She hadn't planned on admitting even that much.

Realizing she'd say no more, he scrubbed a hand down the harsh, rugged plains of his face. "You know I'll warn Falon, right? I'll tell him what's going on."

"Like that scares me." Glory *wanted* Falon to know she was gunning for him. She wanted him to be scared, to tremble and jump at every snapping twig in the night. Hell, maybe she *was* a wicked witch, because she chuckled every time she thought of him dropping to the ground in a fetal ball and crying for his mother.

Sure, he was six feet four of solid—delicious—muscle. Sure, he'd kicked more ass in the few years he'd lived in Mysteria than the town's citizens were currently nailing.

And sure, he probably made the creatures of the underworld pee their pants in fear of him. A girl could dream, though.

"Now." She rubbed her hands together. "Evie, my revenge, if you please. I've tried to bring it up several times, and you ignored me, ran from me, or let your boy toy sweep you off your feet. Literally. I'm not waiting anymore!"

"Whatever he did, I'll talk to him," Hunter said. "He'll apologize."

Glory shook her head, long hair slapping her across the face. It was too late for that. "*I'll* talk to him. Evie . . ."

"Fine." Frowning, Evie uncurled from her lover's body and rose from the bed, taking the sheet with her.

Cheeks heating, Glory quickly turned and faced the hallway. She so had not needed to see Hunter's crowning grandeur. Did she appreciate it? Yeah. Boy was blessed! Still. Her sister's boyfriend was not meant to be eye candy for her, and besides, she didn't need to add fuel to the fire of her constantly unsatisfied desires.

Behind her, she heard cloth rustling, the slide of a drawer, then things bumping together.

"Ah, here it is!" her sister said.

Footsteps sounded, then a delicate finger was tapping Glory on the shoulder. Heart pounding excitedly, she turned. Of course, her gaze flew to Hunter of its own accord hoping for another peek. He'd already tugged on a pair of jeans—jeans with a missing top button. Evie had probably bitten it off.

Glory's chest started hurting again.

Evie waved a black pen in front of her face. "Hello. You paying attention to me?"

Her gaze latched onto the pen, following its movements. Her frown returned. "You're giving me a pen? A *pen* to finally claim revenge against the man who savagely wronged me?"

"Yes. How did he wrong you?"

She ignored the question. "What, I'm supposed to draw a mustache on his picture? News flash. That's not going to leave him crying in his cornflakes."

"Why do you want him crying in his cornflakes?"

Grrr! "No matter how many times you ask, no matter how many ways, I'm not telling."

"Well, don't make him cry too hard. He's a good man and has always been nice to us."

Nice? Nice! Evie had no idea the cruelty that man was capable of. But revealing what he'd done to her would be more mortifying than, say, finding one of her sisters naked and in bed with a vampire, screaming his name as she climaxed.

"Pay attention, sister dear." Evie released the pen; it didn't fall. It hovered in the air between them, swirling, glitter falling like raindrops around it. "This little pen is magical."

"Rock on! What will it do?"

"Anything you write with it will come true."

Glory's eyes widened, the words sinking in. "*Anything* I write will come true?"

"Yes. Well, anything physical, nothing emotional. Just be careful. The more you write, the more ink you'll use, and there's no way to refill it. Also, the effects don't last forever, only for a few hours. For proper revenge, it's best to write about clothes disappearing right off a body in the middle of a crowd and—"

"Don't help her," Hunter growled.

"Yes, but *anything* I write comes true?" Glory asked again, just to be sure.

Evie rolled her eyes. "Physically, yes. I said so, didn't I?"

A laugh escaped her, her first true laugh in months. "Oh, this is classic. Truly perfect."

"I knew you'd appreciate the irony."

"What irony?" Hunter sat up and propped himself against the headboard.

"Can I tell him?" Evie asked her.

Why not? "Sure. He's almost family, and I've seen his goods."

"She's a novelist," Evie threw over her shoulder, "best known for bringing her heroes to their knees. Not always because they fall in love, but mostly because the villains always jack them up with a hammer to the tibia."

"I need help" Hunter mumbled. "This is bad. Real bad."

Glory rubbed her hands together. Yes, it was. Falon the bastard was about to fall. Hard-core!

Two

Anticipation hummed through Glory for the rest of the night and the following day, possibilities rolling continually through her mind. She'd hoped Hunter would tell Falon what was going on, Falon would rush to her and beg her to forgive him, and she would get to slam a door in his face, causing him to toss and turn for hours in fear.

But he never showed up.

So when the sun finally descended on the second day, she padded to her bedroom, wading through clothes, shoes, and donut wrappers, grabbed a notebook, and climbed onto the bed.

It was time to test the pen's powers.

Ever since Falon had—*Do not think about that right now! You know better.* Already, with that tiny half thought, her pulse had kicked into overdrive, and her stomach had clenched, sickness churning inside of it.

Think about your revenge. For this to work, she needed to be strong, unemotional. Otherwise, she'd do something mean, Falon would look at her with those otherworldly violet eyes of his, and she'd cave. Maybe even apologize. *He deserves to suffer.*

How best to torture him?

She thought about what she knew about him. She'd never slept with him, but she knew what he looked like when he experienced ultimate pleasure. She knew how he tensed, knew his voice dripped harsh and raspy. Knew he roared with the last spasm, pounding his big, hard body into his lover's.

Uh, not helping. Breath burned in her lungs, and fire rushed through her veins, but she couldn't stop her mind from traveling that road. One night she'd stumbled upon Falon in the woods, making love to one of his many women. Or, as Glory liked to call them, one of his many hookers. Anyhoodles, she'd been unable to walk away. He'd been unnaturally beautiful and darkly seductive, whispering the most erotic nothings in the hooker's ear.

Glory had suddenly understood why Falon could fight vampires and demons for hours and hours without breaking a sweat. He was total strength, inexorable stamina. *Nothing* tired him.

That night, she'd developed a tiny—enormous—crush on

him. Even though he was way out of her league. Glory was a wee bit on the pudgy side, while Falon personified perfection. She exercised by riding her bike into town to buy a bag of Doritos; he worked out slaying his enemies without thought or hesitation. Men ignored her; women flocked to him. She spent hours in front of a computer, living life in her mind; he actually lived. Inside other people's pants, but whatever.

Rumor was he knew what a female craved before even she knew, and anyone who experienced the bliss of his sometimes gentle, usually savage touch was never the same again. Watching him, Glory had begun to believe that.

She'd fallen completely under his spell, haunted for days by his mesmerizing image. She'd yearned to have him in her bed. In her shower. On her floor. Wherever. She hadn't been picky. She'd just wanted him. Desperately and unequivocally. She'd wanted him naked, slipping and sliding into *her*, no one else, wrapped around her, cherishing her. She'd wanted her name on his lips, his taste in her mouth. Until . . .

Her hands clenched into fists. *You aren't supposed to think about this!*

The memories flooded her, anyway. A few months ago, she'd overheard him tell Hunter that one woman was the same as any other, and love was for idiots. Since they shared the same mind-set—love sucked giant elephant balls!—and he didn't care who he slept with, she'd decided to go for it and throw herself at him.

Pleasure was seriously lacking in her life, and she would have given all of her powers—well, rather, all of *Evie's* powers—to have him look at her with desire. Just once. That's all she'd needed, all she'd wanted.

So she'd gone to his house in nothing but a trench coat and heels. And yeah, she'd flashed him.

He'd taken one look at her and laughed. Laughed!

"Go home, little girl," he'd said. "You don't know what you're playing at."

"I'm twenty-three, not jailbait, and I'm anything but little, as you can clearly see. I'm here for a few hours of fun, that's all."

"Okay, let me put this another way. Get lost. You're not welcome here."

"I'm—I'm not your type, then," she'd stammered, mortified to her very soul. In that moment, she'd understood. Even though he'd said any woman would do, he'd meant any *pretty* woman would do.

His gaze had become hard as it perused her. "No, you're not my type."

He could have spared the remaining tatters of her feminine pride, but another woman had walked up behind Glory. Kaycee, a girl who had graduated a few years ahead of Glory, had obviously craved the same thing as Glory, despite the fact that she'd come with a basket of fruit to "sell." Just as she'd been in school, Kaycee had been tall and thin and pretty. And Falon had allowed that pink-skinned *married* fairy hooker inside before shutting the door in Glory's red-hot face.

Remembering, Glory gnashed her teeth together. "I will destroy his male pride," she said, determined. "I will teach him what it's like to feel unwanted and ugly."

But she spent the next hour staring at the notebook, mind blank. Shit! How did a girl teach a man that kind of lesson?

Just write something. Anything! Pretend this is one of your novels and test the pen's powers. Let's see, let's see. Roman solider? No. Falon didn't deserve to carry a sword. But she saw all kinds of possibilities in that time period. Gladiator? Oh, yes, yes, yes. Gladiators were slaves, and she really liked the idea of Falon in chains.

Closing her eyes, she pictured Falon pacing the dirt floors of a barred cell, sweat rolling down the sculpted muscles of his bronzed stomach, pooling in his navel and dipping lower. Fresh from fighting, blood splattered him.

Licking her lips, Glory shifted against the covers. The scene continued to open up in her mind, painting her thoughts with its descriptions. She sucked in a deep breath and forced her hand to write what she saw . . .

FALON was lying in bed, cool, dry, staring at the ceiling of his bedroom one moment and inside a dirt-laden cell the next, pacing back and forth, sweat pouring from him. Shocked at the sudden change, he tried to stop. His feet kept moving as though they were no longer connected to his brain.

What the hell?

Moonlight slithered around him as he passed a crudely crafted bed, then an equally crude bench, kicking dirt with his sandals. *Sandals?* There was a metallic tang in air. The rustle of chains could be heard beyond the cell, as could moans of . . . injured men? Pleasured men?

Confusion slithered through him.

"Yo. Falon."

Hearing the husky female voice, he spun and faced the cell's farthest set of bars. A lone woman stood behind them, shadows covering her face. Glistening white cloth draped her, and gold flowers glinted from her left shoulder and hem. A chain belt circled her waist, cinching the drape around her and revealing slender curves. The scent of pampered, eager woman and desire drifted from her, sweet and exotic.

His body hardened in hated desire. Hated, because only one woman had that effect on him lately.

"Glory Tawdry," he said through clenched teeth. "I should have known."

"Sweetness, it worked!" She clapped her hands, and he could easily imagine her smiling that sultry, white-toothed smile of hers. "I hope you don't mind, but I decided to write myself into the scene."

"Scene What scene?"

"This one." As she spoke, she stepped into a ribbon of that golden moonlight.

He couldn't help himself. He sucked in a heated breath and drank her in. Long, red hair framed her pretty face—the most sensual face he'd ever seen. Her eyes were large emeralds flecked with gold. Her nose was gently sloped, her cheeks pink and perfectly rounded. Her lips were luxuriant and red, utterly magnificent—but they would have looked better moving over his body.

You know better than to think like that, you walking penis! "What do you mean, you wrote yourself into the scene? What is this place? How did you get me here?"

Her sculpted brows rose. "Didn't Hunter tell you?"

"Tell me what? I haven't spoken to him in days." His friend had stopped coming to Knight Caps, the bar he owned and where Falon bartended, preferring instead to spend every moment with his revenge witch. Disgraceful, if you asked Falon.

"Evie must have distracted him," Glory said with a laugh. "Damn, but I do love my sister."

That laugh . . . it was magical. Almost melted his fury. Almost. His gaze circled the cell. "What have you done to me, Glory?"

"Nothing much. Yet. This is just a small taste of my revenge."

Revenge. He didn't have to ask why. The night she'd

come to his house, flashed him every one of her spectacular curves, and nearly felled him, he'd resorted to the only thing capable of saving him: cruelty.

His gaze met hers, and something hot filled his veins. This time, it wasn't fury. She looked utterly pleased with herself, and the look was good on her. Good enough to eat. She must have sensed the direction of his thoughts because she backed up a step. A pause stretched between them, layered with awareness. Sizzling with need.

There was something about her that appealed to the beast inside him. Something dark, dangerous, and bone deep that awakened urges inside him he'd thought long dead. Tender urges, savage urges.

Do not think like that, idiot! He'd made the mistake of willingly dating a witch twice. Once because he'd wanted the woman, once because he'd needed the woman. Both experiences had scarred him for eternity. The relationship with the first, Frederica, had not ended well, and the damn woman had cursed him with impotence. And no amount of Viagra or stimulation had fixed the . . . limpness.

Falon had been forced to give up a year of his life acting as a slave to Penelope, the second witch, to win his freedom. In return, Penelope had challenged Frederica, who quickly lost and finally reversed her spell. Had the return of his manhood been worth it? He wasn't sure. Penelope had not been an easy mistress. He'd cooked, cleaned, run errands, supplied her with orgasms and massages, balanced her checkbook, punished her enemies, and fixed her TiVo. So yeah, he hated witches! They always abused their powers.

That hadn't stopped him from wanting Glory, though—who was now in the process of abusing her powers! Yes, he'd hurt her all those months ago. But he'd had to push her away before he'd caved.

Still, he'd regretted it ever since and had even tried to make it up to her, acting as her protector on several occasions. "I don't desire this," he said.

"Yes, you do."

"No, the hell I don't! That night in the cemetery, I saved you from hungry corpses." He wasn't sure how or why, but since that night on his porch he always seemed to know when she was in trouble. A fierce surge of protectiveness would rise inside him, and the next thing he knew, he'd be rushing to get to her, wherever she was.

Maybe she'd cast a spell on him.

He bit the inside of his cheek until he tasted blood. That made sense. He should have realized it sooner, but he had been consumed with thoughts of her naked. He wanted to curse at her but held back the words. No need to provoke her. Yet. Damn, what should he do?

Before that fateful night, he'd always avoided looking at her and her witch sisters. Had left a building the moment they'd entered it. Because one glance at that sensual face of Glory's, and he nearly forgot his no witch rule.

Rejecting her that night on his porch had been one of the

hardest things he'd ever done. Literally. She'd been naked. But he'd managed to do it—and he'd done nothing but dream about her ever since.

"What kind of spell is this?" he demanded.

"Don't you worry your pretty little head about that," she said with a sugar-sweet tone. "You worry about the pain and suffering I'm about to rain upon your life."

"Glory—" He pressed his lips together. *Do not antagonize her, or she'll make it worse. Duh.* He raked his gaze over her, trying to decide what to do. Wait. She looked . . . different. His head titled to the side as he frowned. "What did you do to yourself?"

"I wrote myself in as a glorious one hundred and twenty—" Now *she* frowned. A moment later, she disappeared as if she'd never been there.

"Glory?" He spun around, eyes roaming. Where the hell was she?

A moment later, she reappeared in front of the bars. And she looked even thinner, the robe bagging over her bony body. He didn't like it. He liked her curves and the lusciousness of her breasts, hips, and thighs. Even thinking of them caused his mouth to water. Was his tongue wagging?

She smiled. "I wrote myself in as a glorious one hundred and *fifteen* pounds."

"You're skin and bones."

"I know. Isn't it great?" She didn't wait for his answer

but twirled, her smile never fading. Material danced at her ankles like snowflakes. When she stopped, her eyes narrowed on him, and she added tightly, "What do you think of me now?"

He decided to be honest. "I liked you better the other way," he said, crossing his arms over his sweaty, bloody chest—still having no idea how he'd become so sweaty or so bloody.

At first, Glory appeared stunned by his admission. Then her eyes narrowed even more, becoming tiny slits that hid those beautiful hazel irises completely. "Yeah. Right. I've seen your harem. You always pick the skinny ones."

Actually, the skinny ones always picked him, and after a year without being able to get Little Fal up, he'd taken what he could get, when he could get it. Except for Glory. Why'd she have to be a witch?

"Where are we?" he asked.

Her lips curled into a slow, sensual grin, and his stomach tightened. "This is your prison."

He ran his tongue over his teeth. "Why?"

"We already covered this."

Yeah, they had. "Look, I'm sorry about that night. I wish it had never happened."

"But it did happen. Makes sense, though, that you're sorry *now*." Rage crackled around her, lifting strands of her hair as if she'd stuck her finger into a light socket. A moment passed while she calmed herself down, and her hair smoothed out. "I should have written myself inside the cell with you so I could torment you with my superhot bod, but I didn't want you to have access to my neck."

"So that's how you plan to punish me, is it? Magically transport me into a cell and make me horny? By all means, keep at it." He could imagine worse things.

"Oh, no. I plan to do much, much more than that." She licked her lips and perused him, gaze lingering on his stomach, between his legs. That gaze devoured him, eating him up one tasty bite at a time.

Clearly, she still wanted him.

His first thought: *Yes!*

His second: *No, no, no!*

"Don't look at me like that," he growled, not caring if she tried to punish him further. He could not allow this witch to desire him like that. Not when his resolve teetered so precariously. Look what had happened already. Any more . . . No. No way could he allow himself to have her.

Glory's eyes snapped to his, embarrassed hazel against furious violet. "I'll look at you however I want! You're my property right now. I own you."

"Stop this, Glory."

"Make me."

Very slowly, purposefully, he moved toward her.

Approaching her is dangerous, common sense said.

No other way, Little Fal replied.

Glory's mouth opened all the wider with every step he took, but no sound emerged from her. When he reached the bars, he whipped out his arms before she had a chance to stop him and clamped his fingers around her wrists.

"What are you doing?" Her tone lacked any heat, and she actually pressed herself into the bars until her body brushed his. "I didn't add this to the scene."

The contact, though light, sparked a jolt of pure fire in his bloodstream. Up close, she was even lovelier. Freckles were scattered across her nose. Her pale skin glowed with health and vitality.

"You want me to touch you? Is that what it's going to take to get you out of my life?" He anchored her arms behind her back with one hand and traced his other down the front of her robe. How he longed to linger over the small mound of her breasts, the hollow of her stomach . . . the waiting valley between her legs.

If she'd possessed her usual curves, he knew he would not have been able to resist. Her desire to be thin was actually a blessing. But even now, like this, his control wasn't what it should have been. He was freaking trembling.

"Stop," she whispered. Her eyes said *more*.

All of his muscles bunched in reaction to that pleading tone, that needy expression, hardening, aching. He did not stop. He eagerly learned the length of her legs, her skin smooth and soft, like velvet. By the time he finished the full-body caresses, sweat beaded over his face and dripped in rivulets down his chest.

"More." She closed her eyes, all pretense of resistance gone.

He pinched several strands of her hair between his fingers, enjoying the silkiness. He brought the tendrils to his nose and sniffed. Nearly moaned. A fresh, blooming garden. That's what her hair smelled like. He could have breathed in the scent forever.

"If you want me to fuck you," he said, deliberately cruel, just as before, "you'll have to enter the cell." *For the best.* It was better to be punished than to cave, he decided.

"Wh-what?" Her eyes blinked open. He saw the need burning there, the want. Her nipples were hard, visible through her robe. The scent of awakened passion wafted from her, blending with the flowery fragrance of her hair.

"You heard me."

"No, I hate you." The words were spoken on a breathless sigh. Then she shook her head, eyes narrowing again, and backed away. "I'm going to make you want me, Falon. I'm going to make you crave me. But you are never going to have me. Do you understand? Never."

A moment later, she vanished. The prison shimmered before disappearing, too, and the next thing Falon knew, he was lying in his bed again. As the cool sheets met his clean, dry skin, he rolled from the mattress and stalked to his closet.

Fury, desire, and determination pounded through him. He strapped weapons all over his body, dressed, and stalked from his house. No way he'd allow Glory to use her powers against him. Not again.

He was going to find her. Whatever he had to do, he was going to stop her.

Three

HEART thundering in her chest, Glory kept her eyes squeezed shut and inhaled deeply. The first thing she noticed was how the air no longer smelled of decadent man, sweat, and dark spice. Now she caught the faint drift of powdered sugar and jasmine incense.

Who would've thought she'd mourn the loss of sweaty-man air?

Time to check out the rest. Slowly she blinked open her eyes. Her notebook came into view. Everything that had happened was right there, the words staring up at her. She quickly looked away, not wanting to be reminded of her near capitulation. All Falon had done was touch her and she'd forgotten her need for revenge. The feel of his hands on her body, exploring . . . the sound of his rough voice in her ear, whispering . . . the desire blazing in his eyes, beckoning . . .

Her stomach tightened, and the ache she'd experienced inside the prison renewed between her legs. *Keep looking.*

Her flat-screen computer came into view, followed by the wall of magazine pictures she used for references and her *Hunks of the Month* calendar. Trash and dirty clothes were scattered all over her carpet. She hadn't cleaned since that terrible night; she didn't know why.

"It worked," she said, just to break the silence. "It really worked."

She'd actually sent Falon to an ancient prison, *then* she'd actually followed him there. *Oh . . . my.* She sagged against the mattress and closed her eyes again. Falon's image filled her mind. His eyes, an exotic, come-to-me violet fringed by thick black lashes. His dark hair, a little long. The shadowy stubble that dusted his jaw. The bronzed skin and bodybuilder muscles she'd almost held.

The man had exuded a potent animal magnetism; it had oozed from his pores.

What was he doing right now? Cursing her to the heavens? She laughed, delighted by the thought. He might even be tugging on his clothes, determined to race over here and punish her.

She stopped laughing.

Having trouble catching her breath, Glory scrambled out

of the bed. Her jeans and panties floated straight to her ankles. What the hell? Frowning in confusion, she grabbed them, jerked them up, and launched forward. Almost tripped as the clothes tumbled again. Growled. She needed to leave the house, like, now, and the wardrobe difficulties weren't helping. As she bent to retrieve her stuff, the notebook slid out of her fingers and onto the floor.

She released her clothes and reached out. Her eyes widened as she caught a glimpse of her hand. She was so . . . skinny. Her arm was slender, the bones fine. Her fingers were elegant. Wow. No wonder her jeans no longer fit.

Why hadn't her slenderness faded with the scene?

The answer hit her, and she grinned. She'd written it a little later. For the next few minutes, she'd be a total babe.

Seriously, she'd never looked hotter. Maybe she should wait here. Maybe she should allow Falon inside. Maybe, as she'd hoped, he would be overcome with lust for her and the real revenge could begin. He would beg her to sleep with him, and she would say, "Hell, no."

And what if you plump up right before his eyes, huh? What then?

Shit! Glory's heart jolted into hyperdrive, and she raced throughout her room, kicking off the too-big jeans and panties and jerking on a nightgown. The silky pink material bagged on her, but it was the only thing that would cover her *and* stay put.

Why was she so nervous, anyway? There was nothing Falon could do to her. Not while she owned the pen. *Uh, he could steal it and use it against you.*

A knock sounded at the front of the house.

Her mouth fell open, and she straightened. No way. No damn way he'd made it here so quickly. She looked at her bedroom door, turned, and craned her neck to see out the room's only window. A black SUV sat in the driveway. Damn! He had.

"Glory, Falon's here to see you," Godiva called a moment later, only sounding the slightest bit confused.

"Tell him I'm not here." Glory propelled herself over her bed and to the window. She shoved the glass up and out of the way, never letting go of the pen. Cool air wafted inside, ruffling the thin, gaping gown against her skin as she climbed out. The grass was soft against her bare feet.

Maybe she'd go to Candy Cox's, she thought, racing through the night. No, no. Candy's sister was in town or due to arrive in town, and rumor was the woman negated powers of every kind. Worse, Candy's shape-shifting werewolf boyfriend would be there, which meant more sickening PDA.

She could go to Pastor Harmony's. Ugh, no, she decided next. Harmony was now a mother. The Desdaine triplets, then? No. The brats were likely to welcome her inside and secretly call Falon and alert him. So where did that leave her?

"Oh, no you don't," a male voice boomed behind her.

She gasped, panic infusing her every cell. Goose bumps

broke out over her skin. One backward glance—*Shit!* He'd jumped out her window and was now moving toward her, menacing purpose in his every step. His eyes were narrowed on her.

The forest was a hundred feet in front of her. If she could just—a rock cut into her bare foot, and she fell. Grass padded her landing, but the hard impact still managed to shove the oxygen from her lungs.

"Glory," he said, sounding concerned.

"Go home." She grabbed a long, thin stick as she jumped to her feet. Ouch, ouch, ouch. Might come in handy. She jetted forward, taking stock. Heart: still beating. Pen and stick: still in hand. Legs: workable. Aching, but workable. Twigs and rocks continued to scrape into her feet. *Worry about the pain later.* She just needed to get far enough away from Falon to write him into chains. If not . . .

"I called Hunter," Falon shouted, closer to her.

She yelped but didn't allow herself to look back. Already, his masculine scent wafted around her. *Faster, woman!*

"I want that pen, Glory."

Shit! He was even closer now. There was no time to hide. As she ran, branches slapping at her, stinging, she began writing on her arm. *Twigs reached out and grasped at Falon.* The words were barely legible.

Behind her, Falon growled. The rustle of trees echoed through the night.

Was it working?

Several of those twigs caught him and jerked him to a stop.

An animalistic snarl erupted. "Glory!" This time, Falon's voice carried on the wind. He sounded a good distance behind her. "Stop."

Glory slowed her steps. Panting, she tossed a look over her shoulder. Her eyes widened, and she ground to an abrupt halt. Limbs had indeed caught Falon. They were wound around him like bands of indestructible silk, anchoring him to the base of a tree. His lips peeled back from his teeth, and he scowled over at her.

"Come here," he shouted. "Now."

Despite her wheezing, she was feeling very smug. She turned away from him. One push of her fingers, and she broke the stick she'd grabbed when she'd fallen in two.

"What are you doing? Get over here!"

She gripped the hem of her nightgown and tied the pen inside it. Hopefully, if Falon managed to escape, he would confiscate the stick, thinking it was the pen. That done, she turned back to him and approached, waving the stick smugly.

Her muscles were sore from that run, and as she walked, her arms, legs, and waist began to fill out, the weight returning. Her breasts swelled, stretching the fabric of the nightgown. At least the pen stayed in place.

Still, some of her smugness disappeared. She didn't want

Falon to see her like this, but she wasn't going to waste any ink making herself skinny again. Not now, at least. Right now he was too furious to experience desire, no matter what she looked like.

When she reached him, she hid her arms behind her back, as if keeping "the pen" out of his reach. Strands of her red hair blustered forward, stroking his face.

His pupils dilated, black swallowing violet. "You can escape tonight, but I *will* find you. And when I do, I'm going to take that pen and make you wish you'd never met me."

She leaned forward, as though she planned to reveal a big secret. "I already do wish I'd never met you." His warm breath fanned her cheek, a tender caress, and she had to jerk away from him before she did something stupid. Like suck on his earlobe.

Their gazes locked together, a tangle of emotions.

"Look at you," she said and *tsked* under her tongue. "At my mercy."

He raised his chin. "It won't always be this way."

"Like I want to keep you in my life that long. *Always*. Please." She snorted. "A few weeks should do it."

"You think I'll pretend it never happened? Leave you alone afterward?"

"Well, yeah." She arched a brow. "Unless you want more of me."

His eyes narrowed to tiny slits. His features were calm, but the pulse at the base of his neck hammered wildly. "More of you . . . interesting choice of words." Wind danced between them as his gaze perused her.

Her nipples hardened, and she barely restrained herself from covering them with her hands. Instead, she raised her chin and dared him to say something about her weight. She was surprised when he bit his lower lip, as though he was imagining her taste in his mouth—and liked it.

"Witches should have a code of honor, preventing them from hurting others," he said softly.

"Here's an idea. I'll draft up a witches' code of honor, and you draft up a how to reject a woman nicely code of conduct. Sound good?"

Shame colored his cheeks.

Gold star for me. Now drive the point deeper. "Let me tell you a little something about me, Falon. I have never had much self-esteem. My sisters are tall and slender, and men have always drooled over them. But not me. Not chubby Glor." She laughed bitterly. She loved her sisters more than anything on this earth, but they were so perfect, so pretty, that she, who was already vapor, became *nothing* in comparison. "In the span of five minutes, you managed to destroy what tiny bit of feminine pride I had."

His shoulders flattened against the trunk, his eyes closed, and he drew in a breath. "I admit it. I handled the situation wrong."

"Yes, you did. You didn't have to laugh at me. You could have simply said, 'No, thank you.'"

"I wasn't laughing at you. Not really. I just wanted to ensure you never came back. Wait. That sounds just as bad. Look, the truth is, sending you away had nothing to do with your appearance."

"Oh, please."

"It didn't." His lids popped open, and he was suddenly staring at her with such intensity she had trouble breathing. "You're a witch."

There was so much hatred in his voice, she stumbled back. "Yeah. So?"

"So, let's just say I'm not very fond of witches."

She snorted, refusing to believe him. "You've always been nice to Godiva and Genevieve."

"I wasn't . . . attracted to them." The admission was snarled, more an accusation than anything.

"That's—" Wait. What? He was attracted to her? Pleasure zoomed through her with such potency she almost fell to her knees. But the sensation lasted only five seconds before common sense reared its ugly head. *He'll say anything to soften you. Even a humiliating lie.* Pleasure morphed into searing fury.

Why, that . . . that . . . bastard! Her fingers tightened around the stick, and she had to fight the urge to grab the pen and write a hungry lion into the scene. "So you were attracted to me, were you?" she asked as calmly as she was able.

"What do you think?" he muttered, motioning to his dick with his chin.

She dropped her gaze, staring between his legs with wonder. Okay. Maybe he hadn't been lying. He was hard, his erection straining against his jeans. "Th-that's not because of me." Was it?

"Your nipples are hard, and I can see the outline of fine red hair between your legs. Obviously, you're not wearing any panties. So yeah, it's because of you."

Her mouth floundered open and closed. "Only because I'm the only woman present and you're probably in heat." Warmth bloomed in her face as she finally covered her breasts with one arm and between her legs with the other. "So you can just look away!"

"Make me."

"I'll take away your sight. Just see if I won't."

Finally his gaze snapped back up to her face. "Are you truly that cruel?"

Damn him! He'd zapped her anger with those words, making her feel like the wicked witch Evie had teased her about being. "No. I won't go that far," she whispered, as shamed as he'd been a moment ago.

"How far *are* you going to take it, then?"

She peered down at her bare feet—*Ick, time for a pedicure*—and kicked a rock with the tip of her toe. "I honestly don't know."

FALON clenched his jaw, cutting off any words that might try to escape his mouth. A mouth currently watering for a taste of the woman in front of him. Her curves were a thing of beauty. And with ribbons of moonlight seeping from the canopy of treetops, paying her flawless skin absolute tribute, with that flame red hair dancing like naughty nymphs around her shoulders and her lips glistening from the sting of her teeth, his beast wanted to tame her beauty.

Except, she now appeared defeated.

He hated seeing her like that almost as much as he hated being bound. Almost. Right now, however, he was too primed to feel anything more than desire. He wanted her to reach out, to touch him, kiss him. Suck him.

He was hard as a damn rock and needed to come.

"The night you came to my house in that trench coat," he said.

Her attention suddenly locked on him and the fire blazing inside him. "The night you screwed that fairy hooker? *That* night?"

Surprisingly enough, her waspish tone delighted him. "Jealous?"

"As if!"

He hadn't invited the fairy, whatever her name was, to his house. He'd met her in town earlier that day, had talked and laughed with her, but hadn't meant to take it further. Hello, she was married. Had Glory not been standing in front of him, he would have sent the fairy away. He liked sex, yes, but he'd never allowed a woman inside his home. They tended to linger, and he liked to do the deed and move on.

In fact, the moment Glory had taken off, he'd sent the pink-skinned fairy packing. Despite the fact that she had offered him apples—off of her body. He hadn't even touched her. Had just stood at the window, peeking out the blinds like a criminal, hoping for and dreading a reappearance from Glory.

He'd been hard then, too, so maybe he should have slept with the fairy. But it had been flame red hair his hands had wanted to tangle in, hazel eyes he'd wanted to stare into, and a soft, plush body he'd wanted to penetrate.

No one else would have done.

Maybe that was why he hadn't been able to have sex these past few months. He felt guilty for how he'd hurt Glory, so his body would no longer allow him to respond to other women. Maybe he needed to sleep with her once—or twice—and build up her self-esteem. She'd feel better about herself, he'd stop feeling guilty for the way he'd treated her, and they could both go on with their lives.

Are you kidding? Are you so hard up you've got to bed a witch? Think of the consequences, idiot! She's nuts now, so how much worse will she be after you've slept with her? What if she didn't want things to end after the sex was over? What if she tried to punish him again?

"Uh, hello?" she said, exasperated.

"What?" he asked more harshly than he'd intended.

She crossed her arms over her chest, drawing the material of her gown tight over her breasts. And nipples. Which were still hard. She was killing him. He could make out the edge of the pen between her fingers, but he couldn't make himself care.

"You mentioned the incident," she said. "Well, what about it?"

He'd had a point, hadn't he? Oh, yeah. "You were aroused when you came to me."

A huffy gasp left her. "No, I was not! I was going to give you a *chance* to arouse me. That's all."

"Please. You flashed me, and baby, you were already glistening."

Her cheeks heated to the same shade as her hair, making her all the lovelier. "You are very close to losing your favorite appendage." Scowling, peering at him hotly, she jerked the hand holding the pen forward and poised it just below his nose.

"Wait, wait, wait," he rushed out. Damn her and her powers! He lost his erection as every reason he hated witches flashed through his mind. "I'm sorry." *But not as sorry as you'll soon be.* "You were cold as ice that night." *You nearly singed me.* "You weren't turned on at all." *The scent of your desire is still imprinted on my brain.*

Slowly, she lowered her arm, expression mollified.

The limbs binding him began to loosen their grip, and he blinked in surprise. Was it possible? With a twist of his wrist, he was free. That easy, that simple, as if he'd never been bound. *He* had to hold on to the limbs to keep them upright. He blinked again, doing his best to hide his elation.

Glory was going to pay. Oh, was she going to pay. First, he had to claim that stupid pen!

"Com'ere," he said as gently as he was able. "Please. I want to tell you a secret."

She shook her head, red curls flinging in every direction. "What kind of secret?" Suspicion danced in her eyes.

He tried to look troubled.

"Tell me like this. No one can hear us."

"I don't want to say it aloud. It's . . . embarrassing."

Several moments ticked by, and she remained in place. Then she sighed and stalked to him, hands fisted on her hips. She was so sure of her prowess—and his weakness. She'd learn . . .

"What?" she said.

Her feminine fragrance wafted to his nostrils, the same aroma she'd emitted that night on his porch. In the cell. She still desired him. He took a moment to simply enjoy. Savor. Crickets chirped a lazy song, and locusts rattled an accompanying, faster rhythm. In the distance, a dog barked. Around them, pink flower petals floated through the air, warm and sweet, each laced with a strong aphrodisiac. He'd heard that Glory had cast a love spell over the entire town, and since that day the petals had fallen from the sky like summer snow.

"What?" she demanded again.

"This." He grinned, and snapped his arms closed around her waist.

She yelped.

"Got ya," he said.

Four

SHOCK coursed through Glory, and it was mixed with an insidious thread of desire. Falon had her locked against his hard, hot body so tightly she could feel the frantic beat of his heart. Or maybe that was *her* heartbeat. Her breasts were mashed into his chest, her nipples like hard little points, and every time she breathed, she sucked in the scent of strength and soap and dark spice.

"Nothing to say?" Falon asked smugly.

"Let me go. Now." Trying not to panic, she attempted to lift her arms, attempted to flatten her palms against his chest and push him away from her, but her arms were glued to her sides.

"None of that," he said, latching onto her wrists with

one hand and shoving them behind her. With his free hand, he grabbed the stick. Clearly, he assumed it was the pen, because his grin widened.

"Mine now," he said, and stuffed it into his pants pocket.

Do not smile. "Give it back."

"Make me."

Not knowing how to respond, she ran her tongue over her teeth.

His gaze followed the movement, his pupils dilating.

"What are you going to do with me?" she demanded. Or rather, meant to demand. Her voice was breathless. Again. Her body was trembling—and not with fury. How did he do this to her? Make her want him despite everything that had happened between them?

"I don't know," he answered honestly. "I need to think about it, consider my options. Because I can't allow you to run wild, using your powers against everyone who pricks your anger."

"Yeah, well, before you, I didn't use my powers for bad things."

"So I'm just special?"

"Of course you'd think so." Good. Her voice had substance now. "But the real answer is that you're simply the most irritating person I've ever met." *Kiss me. Let it be a terrible experience so that I never crave it again.*

He leaned down and traced the tip of his nose along the curve of her cheek, leaving a trail of decadent fire. Glory tried not to arch her hips and rub against his erection, but she did and, oh, was he ever erect. Long and thick, hard and smoldering.

He groaned, his eyelids fluttering closed. "Again," he commanded.

Stop. Don't do this. Don't travel down this road. A kiss is one thing. But this . . . Ceasing her gyrations was the most difficult thing Glory had ever done, but she did it.

And suddenly he was eyeing her again, lashes casting menacing shadows over his cheeks and electric gaze piercing her soul. "I'm going to kiss you." It was a promise. "And you're going to kiss me back." It was a rough demand.

"No, you're not." *Please, please, please.* "And no, I'm not." *Impossible.*

"Yes, we are. We have to do something to end the madness."

"Fine. Whatever. Do what you want."

"This doesn't change anything."

"I'm glad you understand that."

"Try to take the pen, and you'll regret it."

"I'll regret it anyway."

He arched a brow. "Do you always have to have the last word?"

"Why, yes, I—"

His lips smashed into hers. Her mouth opened automatically, welcoming him inside. He thrust deep, and his flavor filled her mouth. Drugging, addicting. White-hot. A tingling ache sparked to life in her stomach, then spread to her chest, her limbs. She melted into him.

The iron lock on her wrists loosened. Rather than shove him, she wrapped her arms around him, pulling him closer. Her fingers tangled in his silky hair. His hands were free now, too, and they fastened on her waist, urging her forward and backward, mimicking the motions of sex.

Waves of pleasure constantly speared her. This was what she'd dreamed of since going to him that night, so long ago. His mouth on her, his hands all over her, his body straining against hers.

"More?" he whispered.

She nibbled on his bottom lip. "More."

He reached between them and palmed one of her breasts. His fingers plucked at the hardened nipple. "So perfect."

Moaning, she arched her hips. Exquisite contact. Her head dropped backward, and her long tresses tickled her overheated skin. Had Falon not been holding her up with that arm around her waist, she would have fallen.

No, wait. She was gripping spikes of his hair, tugging them. Hard. A few had already ripped from his scalp and were wrapped around her fingers.

He didn't complain.

She eased closer to him, relaxing her clasp. Her mouth found his neck, and she licked. His skin was a little abrasive, but perfect.

"You're so hot," he said.

"On fire," she agreed. She licked the seam of his lips.

He captured the tip of her tongue and sucked. The hand on her waist slid down . . . down . . . and cupped her ass. As he'd correctly guessed earlier, she wasn't wearing any underwear, and the tops of his fingers teased her most feminine core. She was so wet, she practically dripped between her legs.

"Shit. You're killing me." One of his fingers stroked her clitoris.

A tremor rocked her. *Shouldn't be this good. Not with him.*

Before the thought finished whispering through her mind, her entire world spun. Then cool bark was pressing into her back, and Falon was searing her front. He pinned her arms over her head with one hand and palmed her breast with the other.

"I knew you'd be this good," he growled, not sounding the least bit happy about it.

"Wh-what?" Trying to find her common sense, she blinked open her eyes. When had she closed them? Falon loomed over her. His features were harsh, lined with tension, his gaze a swirling sea of blues, purples, and pinks. How odd. They'd never looked that way before.

His shoulders were so wide, his body seemed to engulf her. Sweat beaded over his sun-kissed skin. He was like an animal whose stomach was rumbling—and he'd just spotted his prey. "Knew it," he finished. "Feared it."

What was he talking about? Feared what? And why wasn't he kissing her? "Falon, I—"

"I want this nipple in my mouth."

"Yes." Please, yes. That still qualified as kissing. "Hurry."

He ripped her nightgown down, revealing both mounds of her breasts. They were large. Overflowing. The nipples were pink, the hardened tips desperate. For a long while, he simply stared down at her.

Glory's cheeks began to heat, and not with desire. Did he like what he saw? He was used to slender women, had once turned Glory away because she wasn't his type. How could she have forgotten?

Embarrassed to her soul, she jerked at his hold, meaning to slide the nightgown back in place. He held strong.

His lips curled in a frown. "What are you doing?"

"Ending this," she said, unable to look at him.

"Be still."

"No."

He increased the death grip on her wrists, and his other hand cupped her chin, forcing her to face him. "Why do you want to end it?"

"Because." Like she'd say it aloud. But maybe that's what he wanted. Maybe that's how he meant to punish her.

Punishment. Of course. How could she have forgotten?

You brought this on yourself. Tears burned her eyes, and her chin trembled.

"What's wrong? You look ready to cry."

"Let me go," she commanded brokenly, focusing on his nose so that she wouldn't have to see those amazing eyes of his and whatever emotion was now banked there.

A moment passed in silence.

"Glory," he said.

Do it; look at him. Get it over with. See his disgust and start to hate him again. Slowly, her gaze lifted. When their eyes met, she gasped. There was a fire raging there. Tension still branched his mouth, and sweat still trickled down his temples. He looked on edge, aroused to the point of pain.

"I think you are the most beautiful creature I've ever beheld. And, like I said, I want your nipple in my mouth, and I think you want it there, too."

She gulped, unable to speak past the sudden lump in her throat.

"I'm going to release your arms. You can push me away or you can urge me closer. The choice is yours."

And just like that, she was free. Her arms fell to her sides. She gripped the tree, and jagged bits of bark cut past her skin. The sting did nothing to dampen her desire. He was so hard and hot against her he was like a brand. The pulse in his neck galloped fiercely. His lips were red and glistening from the kiss.

His chest had stopped moving, she realized. He was holding his breath. Waiting. The knowledge . . . softened her. Was he afraid she'd leave him?

With a shaky hand, she reached out and palmed his erection.

He hissed in a breath.

The tip of his penis had risen well above the waist of his jeans. Actually, the material was so strained, the button had snapped open on its own.

"Trying to torture me?" he croaked. "'Cause it's working."

Was it? She moistened her lips and released him. Was bereft without him in her hand.

Now he moaned.

Despite the warnings trying to slither into her mind, she cupped her breasts and lifted them. "Touch me."

His eyes widened in surprised delight. A moment later, he dipped down and flicked his tongue against one pearled nipple, then the other.

She'd experienced pleasure before, but that had been nothing compared to this. There was an invisible cord from each of her nipples that led straight to her core, as if he were actually thrumming her clitoris while he licked her. This was Falon, the man she'd fantasized about for years. The man whose strength and heat and raw intensity destroyed her defenses and made her crave . . .

Soon she was writhing, couldn't have remained still if the plan had been to pretend she felt nothing for him to undermine his confidence and try to convince him he was lacking. He was not lacking.

He scraped her with his teeth, and she groaned. His fingers caressed a path down her stomach. Her muscles quivered when he paused. Glory felt as though she stood on a precipice, waiting to be pushed over. Would he delve lower, like before, only . . . deeper?

"How did I ever find the strength to send you away?" he asked hoarsely.

Some of the flames inside her dwindled to a crackle, and she almost screamed in frustration. If he kept talking, kept reminding her of their painful history, she might lose her pleasure buzz. "No more talking. You'll ruin it."

A soft chuckle rumbled from him. The tip of one finger traced a circle around her navel, then dipped again, lower this time. Dabbling at the small triangle of hair, tickling. "Nothing could ruin this. You're perfection."

Her? Perfection? Entranced, she parted her legs, giving him all the access he could possibly need.

Through the material of the nightgown, he circled her clitoris next. Again. Finally. He pressed.

"Oh, bright lightning," she gasped.

"Like that?"

"Yes. More."

He didn't give it to her but continued to play with her, revving her to that sense of uncontrollable desire again. "You're so wet," he praised. "For me."

"Yes. You." She tried to arch into his touch, tried to force his fingers to press harder. "Falon."

"Oh, but I like the sound of my name on your lips." His tongue glided up to her collarbone, his teeth nipping along the way. She turned her head aside, and he sucked at her pulse.

"I want to get on my knees. I want to taste between your legs. Say yes." He gripped the hem of her nightgown, slowly lifting.

"Ye—" *Red alert!* blared inside her mind, shoving past her need to scream *yes*. If he touched the knot in her gown, he would discover the pen. He would realize he'd taken a stick from her instead.

His knuckles brushed her thigh, and her knees almost buckled. "All you have to do is say *yes*, and my tongue will be inside you . . ."

His dark head, buried between her legs . . . one of her knees, draped over his shoulder . . . his tongue, stroking her to orgasm . . . She yearned for it so badly she had tears in her eyes. But she forced herself to say, "No," and at last to shove him away.

The action was puny, really, but he released her. He was panting, eyes narrowed. She was panting, eyes still burning.

"Things have already gone too far," she managed to get out. *Do I sound as breathless to him as I do to myself?* "This ends now."

He scrubbed a hand over his mouth, his gaze never leaving her face. "Oh, I get it. Punishment received."

He turned and stalked from her, and she wanted to shout that this hadn't been a punishment, not for him, but the words congealed in her throat, and then it was too late, anyway, because he disappeared from view.

Five

FALON fumed for the next three days. For three reasons. (Three must be his new lucky number.) One, Glory had outsmarted him, leaving him with a magicless stick rather than the revenge pen. Two, he hadn't gotten nearly enough of her and had thought about her constantly. And three, she was now ignoring him, as if he didn't matter to her.

He should be happy about that last one.

He wasn't. Damn it, he wasn't!

Motions clipped, he paced through his living room, trying to decide what to do. Like his lack of happiness, this *should* have been a no-brainer: stay out of her life. Never antagonize her again. She'd had her revenge. She'd made him burn, desperate for her, and then had rejected him. They were even. There was no reason they had to deal with each other again. Most likely, bad, magical things would happen if they did.

"As well as hot and sweaty," he muttered. Her passion had been a thing of beauty. She'd writhed against him, her lush body flushed, her hazel eyes blazing. Her breasts had overflowed in his hands. Her skin had been the softest he'd ever caressed. Her long red hair had tumbled down her shoulders and arms, the perfect frame for her exquisite loveliness.

What would have happened if she'd have let him strip her? What would have happened if he'd spread her legs and pounded inside her?

"Heaven, that's what." *But what about afterward?* Would she have wanted more from him or been done with him? Would she have used her naughty magic against him again?

Falon scrubbed a hand over his scalp, nails raking. He was—or rather, had been—crown prince of the Fae. Women had thrown themselves at him, hoping to be queen. None had captured his interest. Then he'd meet Frederica, the witch, and had been entranced. Now he thought, perhaps, she'd used a love spell on him and there at the end it had worn off. But even still, he hadn't hungered for her the way he hungered for Glory. Glory challenged him in every way imaginable.

"Not hard, nowadays," he muttered.

To serve Penelope for the required year in order to gain

his freedom from Frederica's impotence curse, he'd had to relinquish his crown. His brother, Falk, had then taken over. Falk was a good king, respected, admired, and loved. Falon didn't have the heart to take it from him when the year ended. *What kind of king would I make, anyway?* Not a good one, that was for sure. He'd always been too wild.

Besides, over the years he'd managed to carve out a decent life for himself. He didn't need money, but he worked with Hunter at the bar. Amusements abounded, and there was never a dull moment. Brawls, seductions. Plus, it was a hub of information. When people were drinking, they tended to spill their deepest secrets. A few months ago, Falon had overheard three female fairies planning to poison Falk. He'd passed the information on, and the women had been captured in the act, Falk saved.

Falon sighed, his gaze traveling through his home. To thank him, Falk had sent him gifts. Lots and lots of gifts. From plush crimson couches to thick obsidian rugs. From jeweled goblets to a tiered chandelier. While the outside of his modest house might look ordinary, the inside was like a sultan's palace. White lace even hung from each of the doorways. Not his doing. Falk had also sent a decorator.

Falon stopped in front of the velvet sapphire lounge. He pictured Glory splayed across it, naked, her little pink nipples hard. The lamp resting on the marble table beside the seat would be lit, and she would be bathed in a golden glow. She would nibble on her bottom lip, her eyes closed, lashes casting shadows on her cheeks, hand delving down her soft stomach, fingers sinking into the red curls between her legs.

Just like that, he was rock hard. Again.

"Damn it!"

He needed to bed her. Just once. Otherwise, he'd never be able to get her out of his head.

Growling low in his throat, he stalked to the emerald-studded phone. He'd kind of liked his old one, plain and tan, but oh, well. He dialed Glory's number. *This is dumb, this is so damned dumb.* His blood heated at the thought of hearing her sultry voice. What would she say to him?

One of the Tawdry sisters answered on the third ring. "Yeah, hello." She sounded breathless.

"I need to speak with Glory."

"Falon? Is that you?"

"Yes, who's this?"

"This is Genevieve."

"Hey, Evie. I really need to speak to Glory." Before he came to his senses and took matters into his own hands. Literally.

"Is something wrong?"

He closed his eyes and prayed for patience. "Look, is she around?"

"Well, yeah, but I don't think she'll want to chat with you, and maybe that's for the best. She's in a mood."

Evie sounded like that was newsworthy. When *wasn't*

Glory in a mood? "Is something wrong with her? Is she okay?"

"Meaning, did someone physically hurt her? No. You know they'd be dead by my magic if they did."

A warning? "Emotionally, then."

"I don't know. You tell me. Did you kiss her?" Evie asked.

"Who you talking to, baby?" Falon heard in the background.

"Let me speak with Hunter," Falon said.

Crackling static, and then his best friend was saying, "What's going on?"

"Glory okay?"

"Oh, man. She's been stomping around the house for three days, muttering about a stupid kiss, a stupid man, and stupid revenge. She write you into another scene or something?"

"No." But she could do so at any moment, which made him all kinds of an idiot for making this call. And why was she angry? *She'd* rejected *him*. He'd done nothing but try to pleasure her.

"My advice, bro, is to just leave her alone. She'll calm down, and then she'll forget all about you."

That was the problem. Falon didn't want her to forget him. Shit. *He* seriously needed to forget *her.*

"Uh-oh. Here she is," Hunter muttered.

"I'm going for a run," Falon heard her grumble.

"You? Run?" Shock dripped from Evie's voice.

"Well, no one in this household can seem to master magical weight loss, so I'm running the pounds off. You got a problem with that?"

"You don't need to lose weight," he wanted to shout. Then he thought, *She'll be out of the house. It'll be the perfect time to search her room and snatch that pen.* Once the pen was out of her possession, seduction wouldn't be so dumb. A lie, but he didn't care. "Talk to you later, Hunter," he blurted. "Don't tell her I called." He hung up, grabbed his car keys, and stalked into the waiting daylight.

GLORY ran until her lungs felt like they'd caught fire. She ran until her body was shaking from exertion. She ran until her mind was mush. Sadly, none of those things shoved Falon from her mind.

Him and his too-soft lips, his decadent, drugging taste. His hardness, his sweet hands. His final request to taste her. She'd stayed away from him, hadn't even tried to punish him again.

Sweat poured from her as she stumbled up the porch steps and into her house. Cool air kissed her skin. She propped herself against the nearest living room wall and hunched over, trying to catch her breath. It had taken her a few hours after leaving him in the forest to deduce exactly how he'd convinced her, even for a second, that he truly desired her.

Good thing she'd stopped him. Only two other outcomes had been possible: *he* would have stopped before actual penetration, leaving her gasping and desperate, or, if they'd actually gone all the way, he would have told her how bad she was afterward. He might have laughed at her again.

Her teeth ground together as she straightened. He'd told her she would regret using the pen against him. Now she did. She needed a distraction.

The living room was empty. "Evie," she called. "Godiva."

No reply.

Had they left, or were they in their rooms, getting it on? Glory rolled her eyes and pretended there wasn't an ache in her chest. Probably the latter, the disgusting witches. Did they ever take a break? Legs screaming in protest, she lumbered forward, using the wall as a prop.

Down the hall she maneuvered. When she reached her bedroom door, she waved her hand over the knob, magically unlocking it. The door creaked open, and she stumbled inside, forced to kick past the clothes and food wrappers still scattered across the floor.

"Hello, Glory," a strong, male voice said.

She gasped, frozen in place, gaze searching. Her heart pounded in her chest, nearly cracking her ribs when she spotted the intruder. Falon was splayed out on her bed. His dark head rested on her pillow, his arms propped behind his neck.

He wore a clinging black T-shirt that veed at the neck and jeans that showed off the muscles in his thighs.

"Wh-what are you doing here? And how did you get in?" No. No! He'd seen the national disaster state of her bedroom. Seriously, a bra hung from the lamp beside her bed. Sadly, she looked worse. "Don't look at me," she said, wanting to turn away as his eyes drank her in.

"Why? You're beautiful. I *like* looking at you. Just as you are," he added.

She rubbed her damp palms against her thighs. "What are you doing here?" she repeated, because she didn't know how else to react to his praise. The pleasure she felt was unacceptable.

"I would have pegged you for a neat freak," he said, ignoring her question. Again.

At least he didn't sound disgusted. "So?"

"Where's the pen?" he asked conversationally.

She raised her chin. "Like I'll tell you."

"You haven't used it against me since our . . . the . . . our time in the forest." Had he just stammered? Had his voice dropped with desire?

"Maybe I just haven't thought of the appropriate punishment yet."

One of his brows arched, and he sat up slowly. "Punishment for what? Making you feel good?" Now his voice was dry. "Or not taking you all the way?"

"Just get out." She pointed to the hallway.

He flattened his palms at his sides, his gaze roving over her. That white-hot gaze lingered at her breasts, between her legs, reminding her of everywhere he'd touched—and everywhere he'd wanted to touch. She gulped. She was wearing a white tank top and sweat shorts, and sweat still poured down her flushed skin. She probably looked ridiculous and frumpy.

"Your skin is glistening," he said, and there was enough heat in his eyes to keep her warm all winter. If Mysteria ever got cold, that is.

"Sweat does that to a girl."

"I wish I had been the one to make you sweat."

Now her heart skipped a beat. "What do you want from me, Falon? An apology? Well, you're not going to get one. We're even. I'm done with you."

His eyes sharpened. "You're not done with me. Not until you destroy the pen in front of me."

"No. There's ink left."

"So you plan to use it against me again? You just said we're even."

"We're even *now.* I destroy it, and you're free to torment me for the rest of your life."

He leaned forward, and she caught the scent of soap and

dark spices. Shivered—then shuddered. What did *she* smell like?

"I'll swear not to hurt you," he said.

"And I'm sure you'll mean it. Today. What about tomorrow?"

Growling, he fell back into the mattress and scoured a hand down his face. She noticed he did that a lot when he was frustrated. "I came here to find the pen, but do you know what I really wanted to do?" He didn't wait for her to reply. "I wanted to follow you on your run, make sure you were safe."

Really? How . . . sweet. Some of the ice around her heart melted. *Don't believe him, stupid!*

"I wanted—want—to strip you, make love to you. Finish what we started. I can't get you out of my mind. You're the last person I should want." Now he seemed to be talking to himself. "But want you I do. Maybe if I have you, I can stop thinking about you."

Oh, how she wished. He'd consumed every corridor of her mind since their kiss. Always she craved him. Always she dreamed of him, hungered. Sometimes she was even willing to toss caution aside and go to him, beg him to take her. But . . .

What would happen afterward?

She had several strikes against her. She was a witch, and he hated witches. He was perfection, and she was the epitome of *im*perfection. She'd spent the last week torturing him.

Three strikes. You're out, girl. Glory sighed. She was afraid she'd already fallen for him, though. He was strength, and he was courage. He hadn't backed down from her once, even though her powers were considerable, and she could do major damage to him. His kisses were the best thing to have ever happened to her. His touch, electric. Finally she'd gotten a glimpse of what Evie and Hunter, Godiva and Romeo must experience every night. And different hours through the day. She'd liked it, wanted more.

Wanted him.

"No response?" he said, cutting through the silence.

She shook her head in hopes of clearing it. "You're willing to have me now?"

"I was willing before. I just fought against it."

"But you're not fighting now?"

"No. I can't." He rolled to his side and stared over at her. "I'm helpless. Did you cast a love spell on me?"

"No!"

"I didn't think so," he muttered. "Hoped, but didn't think."

"Why not?"

"Because a witch did it once, and this isn't the same."

Her shoulders sagged. No love for her, he meant.

"It's more intense," he grumbled, surprising her.

Her legs began shaking more forcefully, and any moment she feared she would collapse. Somehow she managed to stumble to the chair in the corner and plop atop the many

T-shirts heaped there. Falon's gaze never left her. She felt it boring past her skin and straight into her soul.

"You want me, too," he said. Hard, flat. "Don't try to deny it."

As if she could. "Who tried to deny it?"

His lips formed a thin line. Almost a smile, but not quite.

"Look, I came to you once offering the same thing. One night. You rejected me."

"Yes, and it was the biggest mistake of my life."

"Because you were made to suffer for it," she said. A statement rather than a question.

"No. Because I crave you."

Truth or lie? She dared not hope. "Now you're out to protect yourself from me, and that's perfectly understandable, but—"

"I don't need protection from you," he snapped.

"Falon, we'll never be able to trust each other. We'll always suspect each other's motives."

"We can call a truce. I'm not asking for a lifetime. I'm asking for a night. And when you came to me that night, that's all you wanted, too."

"I—I—" *Wanted to say yes,* she realized. Wanted it more than anything. After his kiss, though, she couldn't delude herself and hope the sex would be so bad she'd never desire him again. The sex would be great. At least for her. She *would* want more than a night; she knew that now. He . . . affected her. "I can't," she finally said.

"Damn it. Why?" He shot up again, glaring at her.

If he approached her, if he touched her . . . Tremors racked her, part of her wishing he'd do it. Force her hand. "We bring out the worst in each other."

Surprisingly, that mollified him somewhat. "I don't know. I thought we brought out the best in each other while in the forest."

"That was a mistake."

"My favorite mistake, then."

Dang it, if he kept saying things like that, she'd cave. Already her defenses were cracked. Really, what would one time hurt? Sure, she might fall for him even more than she already had. Sure, she might crave more from him. Sure, he might compare her to every girl he'd ever been with, and she would definitely come out lacking. Sure, this might be a scheme on his part to castigate her for using that pen against him. But she'd have an orgasm, so what did those things matter?

And what if . . . what if he truly desired her? What if he enjoyed being with her?

What if: the most dangerous words known to man.

"I just can't," she forced herself to say. Her voice cracked, just like her defenses. She had to swallow a sudden lump in her throat. "My answer is and will always be *no*. Find someone else."

"You want me to sleep with another woman?" he gasped out, incredulous.

"Yes?" she replied, a question she'd meant as a statement.

"You won't care?"

"No." Her hands curled into fists as rage swam through her bloodstream. She'd destroy anyone he touched. Obliterate anyone he— *What are you doing? Stop thinking like that!* "I can give you a love potion for the woman if you think it'd help." *Idiot! What are you saying?*

I thought I was supposed to push him—oh, never mind. Damage done.

Scowling, he jackknifed to his feet. "You want me to be with someone else, I'll be with someone else. I don't need a love potion to do it, either. See you around, Glory."

Glory watched him stride from her bedroom, heard the front door slam. Her shoulders sagged against the chair, and she covered her mouth with a shaky hand. What the hell had she just done?

· Six ·

HE'D made the boast to see another woman. Now he had to see it through. *Shit,* Falon thought. But if he had to prod Glory's temper until she snapped and used that stupid pen, he'd do it. Do *anything* to have her in his arms again. *What's happened to me?* He'd gone from hating her powers to craving them. He just flat-out refused to be ignored by her any longer.

"I'll give you a love potion," he mocked. He'd seen the jealousy flare in her gorgeous eyes when they'd talked about him dating another woman. Glory hadn't wanted him to sleep with someone else; she just hadn't wanted to admit she desired him for herself. So he'd *make* her do it. Because he had to get his hands on her breasts, had to rub himself between her legs. Had to have her taste in his mouth and her pleasure moans in his ears. *Then* he could hate her magic again. Then he would go back to being a rational male who didn't need anyone in particular.

He massaged the back of his neck. Hopefully, if he worked this just right, he wouldn't earn himself another year of impotence. Hopefully, Glory would write the two of them into a sensual scene, and he would be able to finally, blessedly seduce her.

Who would have guessed he'd be reduced to seducing a witch? Not him, definitely. Yet here he was, at home again and picking up the phone to dial an old lover who was still a friend.

When she answered, he said, "I need a favor. And before you say yes, you should know we'll be dealing with a very powerful and somewhat insane witch."

And then, when he hung up with Kayla, he called Hunter. His best friend answered, and he said, "Look, I need a favor, and you owe me, so don't even think about saying no."

"HURRY, up, Glor!"

"I'm hurrying, swear." The moment Glory had sailed through the front door of their home, her sisters had rushed her into the shower. They'd thrown a tight black dress and lacy lingerie at her when she'd emerged.

Now she was in the process of fitting her body into the sheer clothing. She should use the pen to make herself slender again but didn't want to waste the ink for some silly dinner.

Hunter was taking them to the Love Nest, a five-star restaurant that catered to the affairs of the heart. Gag. She'd rather vomit than go, but Godiva had batted those sweet hazel eyes at her, and she'd found herself agreeing.

Unfortunately, the shower had failed to wash away the trials of the day. Glory had spent six hours in town, hawking her love potions for a little extra spending money. A few times, she'd wondered what she would do if one of the women who'd purchased a vial of Number Nine used it on Falon. Then she'd thought, *If he truly loves someone, no potion will sway his heart.* Then she'd thought, *If he doesn't love anyone, he's fair game.* Which basically meant Falon was fair game.

The knowledge had settled uneasily inside her, made her twitchy. She'd always considered her powers a blessing. For her, for others. Perhaps Falon was right, though. Perhaps she was a danger to everyone around her. But it wasn't like she could forsake her powers. They were a part of her.

"We're going to be late," Evie said, drawing her from her musings.

"So? I think the restaurant will survive."

"So Hunter is a vampire and only has a limited amount of time to play. Hurry."

Glory sighed. "You're right. I'm sorry. Maybe I should stay home. I'm in a terrible mood. Besides, I should be working. I have a book due in a few months, and I haven't written a word."

Now *Evie* batted hazel eyes at her. "You can put it off for another night. Please. For me."

She had no willpower when it came to pleasing her sisters. "Fine. I'll go. What are we celebrating, anyway?"

"The anniversary of the first time Hunter said he loved me."

Trying not to grimace, Glory spun and faced her sister. "Are you freaking kidding me?"

Clueless, Evie shook her dark head. "No."

The two lovebirds celebrated everything! The anniversary of the first time they had laid eyes on each other. The anniversary of the first time they had made love. The anniversary of Hunter's change from human to vampire. It was truly sickening. "Isn't that something the two of you should celebrate alone?"

"We will." Evie's lips curled slowly, suggestively. "Later."

Godiva peeked her pale head around the door. "Ready, sister dear? Oh, my." Her body rounded the rest of the corner, and then she was walking forward, expression warm. "You look gorgeous."

There wasn't a single malicious cell in her oldest sister. The woman was pure gentleness and had always been that way. "I feel silly," she admitted. She faced the full-length mirror.

The black dress flowed gracefully over her hips, gossamer, like a butterfly's wing. But with her arms stretched down at her sides, the hem did not even reach her fingertips. Thin straps held the material in place on her shoulders. A beaded empire waist cinched everything in just under her breasts, before flaring and floating free.

Overall, the dress was a naughty version of a Grecian toga. On her feet, she wore strappy black sandals. Her toenails were painted a vivid shade of emerald.

"You've always been the most beautiful of us," Godiva said.

"Hey." Evie frowned at their oldest sister. "I'm standing right here. What am I, dog food?"

Godiva waved a hand in dismissal. "You've always been the firecracker."

"You've always been the peacemaker," Glory said, "and let's be real. I've always been the—"

"Nope," Godiva interjected, gripping her shoulders and spinning her. "I'm not going to allow you to put yourself down. You are an amazing woman, and it's time you realized that."

Fighting tears, Glory kissed her sister softly on the cheek. "I love you."

"Love you, too."

Evie threw her arms around them with such force, they gasped. "I love you guys, too. Now let's haul ass! And, Glory, bring your pen. You know, just in case."

Everything inside of her froze with dread. "Just in case

what?" Each word was punctuated with warning. Had Evie done something?

"Who knows? It's a beautiful night. Anything can happen."

"I never thought I'd see you like this."

Falon eyed Kayla Smith from across their candlelit table. She was a beautiful woman with pale hair, bright blue eyes, and legs that went on forever. Sadly, she did nothing for him. Not anymore.

She was cousin to Candy Cox, the infamous high school teacher now dating a werewolf; was fully human; and had lived in Mysteria so long she found nothing unusual about vampires, goblins, fairies, or witches. They'd dated on and off for a few months, realized they were working themselves into a relationship, and had backed off. Neither of them had wanted to be tied down. He'd always liked that about her. She was fun and playful and never took anything too seriously. Even men.

But he found himself wondering how Glory had been with past boyfriends. Fun and playful, which he decided he no longer liked? Hopefully, Glory had been miserable with other men. Or had she been serious, which for some reason he liked even less. Fine. He just didn't like the thought of Glory with another man, period.

More, he found that he didn't like the fact that he didn't

know everything about her. Suddenly he yearned to know what she ate for breakfast, what her favorite song was, what she dreamed for her life, if she liked to snuggle and watch movies in bed. And if so, were they romantic comedies or action adventure? Probably slashers.

"Are you listening to me?" Kayla asked him.

No. What the hell had she just said? Oh, yeah. She'd never seen him like this. "Yes, of course I was listening. What way do you think you see me?" he asked, his gaze immediately straying back to the restaurant's front door. Where was Glory?

"On edge for a specific woman." There was laughter in her voice. "By the way, you missed a very scintillating conversation I just had with, apparently, myself about a hot tub."

He waved the hot tub away with a dismissive hand. Although, Glory, wet and naked . . . "I'll get her out of my system." He hoped. "Don't worry." With every minute that passed, he just wanted her more.

How would she react when she saw him with Kayla?

Hopefully—how many things was he hopeful about now?—her sisters had convinced her to bring the pen. Hopefully, she would write them into a bedroom. Maybe chain him to the headboard. Yes, chains could definitely come in handy.

The front door to the restaurant opened. He stiffened, poised on the edge of his seat.

Godiva strolled inside, directly behind her was her boyfriend, Romeo, tall and muscled and very wolfish. Falon's stomach rolled into a thousand different knots. Evie walked in, saying something over her shoulder. A moment later, Glory came into his sights. Finally!

Breath congealed in his throat. She was . . . magnificent. Her long red curls tumbled down her back, and the sheer fabric of her dress swayed over her lush hips and thighs.

Hunter stepped in behind her and approached the hostess. The group was led to a table directly across from Falon's. The closer she came, the hotter his blood flowed. *See me. Want me.*

It was as Glory was helped into her seat that she spied him.

Her hazel eyes widened with shock then narrowed with fury. Or arousal. She licked her lips. Spotted Kayla. Gripped the edge of the table so tightly he feared it would snap in half.

"Wow," Kayla said. "I don't have to ask which one is yours."

His. He liked the sound of that.

"She's the one shooting daggers at us. Or rather, me."

"Right."

He should take Kayla's hand, perhaps kiss it. But he couldn't bring himself to do it. The only skin he wanted to kiss was Glory's.

Her sisters took their places at her sides, and he heard her bark, "Did you know about this?"

Both women nodded guiltily.

"Traitors! Why not ask him and his date to join us, then. I couldn't possibly feel any more uncomfortable."

"Hey, Falon," Hunter called. "Glory would really love it if you and your date joined us."

Glory's mouth fell open. "I was joking. I didn't—"

"We'd love to." He was on his feet a second later, jerking Kayla to hers.

Kayla chuckled softly.

Deep down, he didn't think Glory would turn the heat of her anger on the other woman. After he'd foolishly turned her away that night, she hadn't gone after the fairy he'd allowed inside. Only him. Clearly, she was a smart woman and knew where to properly lay the blame.

A waiter dragged two extra chairs to the table, positioning him and Kayla directly across from Glory. He wanted to be closer but would settle for simply looking at her.

You have it bad, man. You've gone from hating witches to being desperate for one in less than a week.

Strangely, he didn't care anymore. Not while he was soaking her in.

"Since the big guy isn't going to introduce me," Kayla said, breaking the silence, "I'll introduce myself. I'm Kayla Smith."

Everyone introduced themselves. Except for Glory. When it was her turn, she motioned the waiter over and ordered a glass of flaming fairy. Falon nearly choked on his sip of water.

"You know I'm of the Fae. How?" he asked her. Not many people did. He was too big, too much a warrior compared to the usually party-loving race.

Her eyes widened. "You're Fae?"

Okay, so she hadn't guessed. He didn't mind that she now knew; he wanted her to know everything about him. "Yes."

"Why didn't you tell me?" Hunter asked, incredulous.

"No one's business."

Awkward silence followed.

"Well, this is fun," Evie said, probably to break the tension.

"A blast," Kayla agreed. She tossed her hair over one shoulder, revealing sun-kissed skin.

Glory saw the action and popped her jaw.

"I've always had low self-esteem," she'd once told him. Oh . . . shit. Bad move, bringing the ex, he realized. He didn't want Glory to feel bad about herself or think he found Kayla more attractive. "You're the prettiest woman here, Glory," he said honestly.

Her drink arrived, saving her from replying. But her eyes had met his over the candlelight, soft and luminous. Her lashes cast dark shadows over her cheeks. Shadows he wanted to trace with his fingertips.

Menus were thrust at them. Falon didn't bother opening his. He didn't care about the food. He continued to watch Glory, couldn't stop himself. He was entranced. She opened her menu, though she didn't read it. She still watched him, too.

Her cheeks flushed to a rosy pink. She was clearly having

trouble drawing in a breath, her chest rising too quickly and too shallowly.

"Hungry?" he asked her in a low, raspy voice.

Her gaze dipped to his lips. "A little."

"I'm starved."

"Why do I get the feeling they're not talking about food?" Evie muttered.

"Because they're not," Hunter told her, "so hush."

The table fell quiet, all eyes glued to Glory and Falon.

Get your pen, he mentally willed. *Write us away from here.* But she didn't. She finally looked away.

His teeth ground together. He'd just have to push her harder, then. *I'm so pathetic.*

"I decided to take your advice," he said.

Fury curtained her features a split second before she blanked her expression. What thoughts tumbled through her mind? "Is that right?" The words were precisely uttered, as though shoved through the crack in a steel wall and ironed out.

"That's right."

The waiter came to take their order, but Kayla shooed him away. Hunter, Evie, Godiva, and Romeo propped their elbows on the table, unabashed by their staring.

"Funny that it wasn't too long ago you *protested* taking my advice," Glory said.

"Isn't it?"

"It is. I'd like to say I'm surprised, but I can't." She tapped a nail against her glass, and the red liquid swished. "Not if I'm being honest."

His lips pursed. Did she truly think so poorly of him? Of course she did, he thought in the next instant. He'd once told her that he hated witches. He'd once told her that he would pay her back for all she'd done to him.

Worry about that later. When she's naked and under you. Or over you. Right now, you have to push her. "I'm thinking about showing Kayla my favorite . . . gladiator costume. Does *that* surprise you?"

Hunter choked on his water. Romeo nodded encouragingly. Evie, Godiva, and Kayla leaned forward, obviously intrigued.

Glory gasped at the reminder of the night she'd written him into a slave's cell, splattered with blood and fresh from battle.

"I'm learning things about you I wish you'd kept hidden," Hunter muttered.

"Shut it," Falon told him.

"Why don't you show her your jackass costume?" Glory asked through clenched teeth. "Oh, wait. You're already wearing it."

Okay, he'd walked into that one. Had she been talking about anyone else, he would have laughed. He loved her wit. And she must love warriors. Why else would she have written him into such a situation?

He racked his brain for things he knew about ancient

Rome. Not much. Everything he knew, he knew because of Russell Crowe. "For the woman I desire, I would be willing to do anything." The words were a dare, a challenge.

"A few flicks of my wrist, and I can make you prove those words. Violently."

Do it. "Please." He snorted. "You've run out of ink, and we both know it."

She leaned forward, curls spilling onto the table. Oh, she was lovely. "Do you *want* to die?"

"Yes. Of pleasure."

Her pupils dilated, and her nostrils flared. Just then, she was like a living flame, fury crackling over her skin. *I'm close. So close. Just a little more.*

"Maybe you'd like to visit a village of Vikings? Or maybe you'd like to come face-to-face with a Highland chieftain and his sword?"

"If that turned you—her on, then yes."

Glory ran her tongue over her teeth. Every muscle in his body jerked at the sight of that pink tongue. Oh, to have it on *him*.

"It would," Kayla said. "It really would. What do I have to do to get in on this action? I'd prefer a Viking over a chieftain, but will graciously accept whichever you give me."

Slowly, Glory eased back in her seat. Slowly, she grinned, though the expression lacked any type of humor. "I think something can be arranged. For you," she added, eyeing Falon, "not her."

"Please," Kayla said at the same time he said, "Fine. I understand." He was thinking, *Finally!*

As she reached inside her purse, Falon added, "Oh, and Glory?"

"Yes?" Grin feral, she lifted the pen and tapped it against her chin—to taunt him, he wouldn't doubt. Fire still raged in her eyes.

Are you really going to do this? He peered at her heaving chest, her dilated pupils, her lush, red lips. *Hell, yes.* "Since I'm doubting you have the courage to write yourself into the scene, I guess I'll see you when I get back."

Her eyelids narrowed, and she lost her grin.

He barely stopped himself from laughing. *See you there, baby.*

Seven

HE wanted her to write them both into a scene, an oddity on its own. He hadn't seemed to mind the thought of his precious Kayla being given to another man; he had seemed more interested in Glory. Glory knew all of those shocking things, but she didn't understand them.

Why had he fought for magic to be used against him? Why had he antagonized her?

Did the reason matter? she thought next. She was at home, alone in her room, and she was going to use the pen. Not to punish Falon—though she wanted to do so. He'd taken another woman to dinner. A beautiful, slender woman. No, Glory was doing this to be with him, to have him to herself. She'd simply used punishment and anger as an excuse.

When will I learn?

She'd tried to stay away from him. She'd ignored his phone calls, hadn't ventured near his house. She'd even walked out of a room anytime he had been mentioned. She feared falling so deeply in love with him, she'd never recover. As she'd once told him, they could never trust each other. But she was still going to do this. She craved him, and the craving wasn't going away.

Despite all of her reasons for avoiding him before, she couldn't stop herself now. She needed to shove him from her thoughts and dreams, and nothing else had worked. Why not give this a shot and experience another dose of that heady pleasure while she was at it? She'd do her best to guard her heart. Oh, oh. Maybe she could take an antilove potion.

She was nodding as she popped to her feet. Antilove. Of course! There was nothing she could do about the emotions she harbored now. Once there, they were immune to magic. But she *could* prevent herself from falling for Falon completely.

Clothes and trash soared through the air as she crouched on the floor and rooted through them. Every vial she found, she set aside. Love potion Number Nine. Love potion Number Thirteen.

A magic suppressor. A magic unleasher. Ah, finally.

Straightening, she raised a tiny bottle of swirling, azure liquid. There was a warning label in the center.

"Take with food," she read. "May cause dizziness. If you become sick, consult your nearest witch."

She'd given the potion to hundreds of women but had never sampled the goods herself. There'd been no need. The recipe had been designed by her great-grandmother and was now used in every spell book she'd ever encountered. It had to work. No one had ever complained.

"Here goes nothing." Glory popped the cork and drained the contents. Tasteless but smooth. A minute passed. Nothing happened. Another minute. Still nothing. She tossed the empty bottle over her shoulder. Maybe she wasn't supposed to feel anything.

Frowning, she swiped up the pen and a notebook and plopped onto the side of her bed. What was Falon doing right now? Was he at home with Kayla? Waiting for Glory to act?

What was the couple doing to pass the time?

"Grr!"

Unable to wait any longer, Glory began writing: *Falon is alone in his house, unable to leave.* That took care of Kayla. Glory's frown faded. She wouldn't make him battle anyone like he'd suggested. That would make her admire him more. Even the image was dangerous. Falon. With a sword. Her mouth watered.

She'd get straight to the sex. Do him and forget him. *His clothing suddenly disappears, leaving him naked.* As the ink stained the paper, she had trouble drawing in a breath. Her hand was shaking.

Glory appears—

No. She scratched out those two words. Falon was now alone and naked. She couldn't just appear in front of him looking like this.

Glory weighs one hundred and fifteen pounds and is wearing a lacy, emerald green bra and panty set.

One moment she was draped in the black dress her sister had given her, the next, cool air was kissing her bare skin. Glory looked down. Sure enough, her *small*, perky breasts were pushed up by emerald lace. Her stomach and legs were thin and glorious. She grinned and kept writing.

Falon is chained to his bed, and Glory suddenly appears in front of him, pen and notebook in hand.

Glory's messy bedroom faded to black, and then Glory was lying against cool, silky sheets. Cold metal anchored her wrists and ankles in place, her pen and notebook gone. A white chiffon flowed overhead, like a cloud descending from heaven.

"What the hell?" She tugged at her arms. The chains rattled but didn't budge.

Suddenly Falon approached the side of the bed, the pen and notebook in his hands. He looked at Glory, and his eyes widened. He looked at the contraband he was holding, and he grinned.

"It worked," he said, shocked. "It really worked."

Her struggles increased. "What worked? What happened? What did you do to me?" What the hell was going on?

He was naked, and his tanned body was magnificent. Rope after rope of muscle, traceable sinew, and a long, hard erection. A glittering necklace hung from his neck.

She looked away from the sheer majesty of him, struggled some more.

"Be still," he said.

"Go to hell!" The metal began to cut into her skin, drawing warm beads of blood.

Falon *tsked* under his tongue. He strode out of the bedroom, leaving her alone.

"Falon!" she cried. Panic infused every corridor of her body. "Don't leave me like this! Come back."

He returned a moment later, the pen and notebook gone. In their place were strips of cloth. "Be still," he ordered again, sharply this time.

She obeyed. She was panting, skin overly hot. At least he'd covered himself with a robe, blocking all that male deliciousness from her view. "What's going on? How did you do this? You don't have any powers."

He eased beside her, and the mattress jiggled. She tried to scoot away, but the chains didn't allow her to go very far. "No, I don't have powers. But I do have a friend who is dating a witch who wants her sister happy."

Her jaw went slack. "*Evie* helped you?"

Leaning forward and wafting the scent of man and dark spice to her nose, Falon began wrapping the cloth underneath the chains, protecting her skin. *Do not soften.* She'd taken the antilove potion. She shouldn't have to warn herself to remain distant, but the potion wasn't freaking working.

"Hunter questioned Evie about the pen," he finally explained. "Apparently, Evie failed to tell you that she had a charm to counteract the effects of it."

"I don't understand." *Come closer, keep touching me.* She had to bite her lip to keep the words inside.

"Anything negative you wrote about the person wearing the charm would be done to *you* instead."

Shock sliced through her, as hot as he was. "That's—that's—"

"What happened. Hunter also emptied out your potions and replaced them with colored water. Just in case you tried to feed me one."

So that was why . . . "That little jackass!" No wonder the antilove potion hadn't worked. Now she was helpless, on her own. The knowledge should have panicked her all the more. Instead, she found herself praying his robe would split, and she would be able to see his nipples. Maybe lick them.

"I had wondered what kind of scene you would write, and must admit I'm surprised by what you chose. I expected hungry lions or a raging, bloody battle and thought I would have to pluck you from its midst. I'd even draped myself in armor, just in case. Then that armor disappeared and I began to hope . . ."

Her cheeks flamed; they were probably glowing bright

red. She tried to cover her embarrassment by snapping, "Why didn't my clothing disappear instead? Since you have the charm and all."

"The removal of clothing isn't negative." His head tilted to the side, and his gaze roved over her. He frowned. "Why do you write yourself like that?"

"Like what?"

"So . . . thin."

"Because," was all she said. *Because I want to be pretty for you.*

"I like you better the other way."

"Liar. Now write me out of this scene!"

He shook his head. "Hell, no. I've got you right where I've always wanted you. And I'm not a liar. In fact, I refuse to touch you while you're like this. When you're back to normal, *then* the loving can begin."

A tremor rocked her. She didn't dare hope . . . "The chains will disappear by then, too, and if you think I'm staying here, you're crazy."

"You can be rechained."

Good point. "The pleasuring will never begin, because I've decided I don't want you."

"Now who's lying?" He pulled a plush lounge next to the bed and sat, gaze never leaving her. "I'll make a pact with you. I won't lie to you, if you won't lie to me. From now on, we'll be completely honest with each other. Okay?"

"Whatever you say," she said in a sugar-sweet tone.

"So what do you think of my bedroom?"

"It's—" She'd been about to say something mean, but then her sights snagged on the crystal chandelier, dripping with thousands of teardrops. On the intricately carved dresser, orchids spilling from vases. A bejeweled tray provided the centerpiece. "Unexpected," she finally finished.

"Everything inside the house was a gift from my brother."

Her head snapped toward him. "I didn't know you had a brother."

Falon nodded, his hair dancing over his cheeks. "There's a lot you don't know about me, but that's going to change. We're going to get to know each other, Glory."

"No." That would defeat the purpose of loving and leaving. If he continued this, she would leave, but she would not be unscathed.

"Oh, yes," he insisted. "And every time you reveal a fact about yourself, you'll earn a reward."

Goose bumps spread over her skin. "And if I remain quiet?"

Slowly, he grinned. "You'll earn a punishment. I have the pen, after all."

This is not fun. This is not exciting. I am not turned on. "Fine. Tell me how many women you've had in here." There. That should deepen—dampen—her terrible—wonderful—mood.

"You are the first."

She flashed him a scowl. "I thought we weren't going to lie to each other anymore."

"I spoke true. You are the first woman I've ever allowed inside this bedroom."

"What about the fairy? That night—"

He held up a hand for silence. "I sent her home the moment you were out of sight."

Seriously? Glory didn't know whether or not to believe him, but she adored the idea of his claim. "What about Kayla?"

"Sent her home, too. I didn't want her; I wanted you. As you might have guessed, I used her to get your attention."

"Well, you got it," she grumbled, then cringed at the admission.

"I noticed you the first day I moved into town, you know," he said.

He'd noticed her? In a good way? She shivered, feeling as if his hands were already on her, caressing, stoking her desire.

"Cold?" he asked.

She nodded, because she didn't want to admit his words had ignited a storm of desire inside her.

He rose, grabbed the black silk comforter, and tugged it over her. The material was cool against her skin, but damn it, it didn't dampen her need. No, it increased it. Every nerve ending she possessed cried for him.

Falon placed a soft kiss on her lips. Automatically she opened her mouth to take it deeper. He pulled away.

A moan slipped from her.

"Soon," he said as he reclaimed his seat. His voice was tense. "Now, back to the first time I saw you. You were outside with your sisters and selling your potions. At the time, I didn't know they were potions. I just saw a beautiful woman with rosy skin and hair like flame."

She gulped, couldn't speak.

"I wanted you so badly." As he spoke, his fingertip caressed her thigh. "I was making my way toward you when I heard the words 'potion' and 'witch,' and then I couldn't get away from you fast enough."

Maybe he *was* telling the truth about his desire for her. Maybe he did like her just the way she was. Maybe . . .

"I never tortured anyone until I met you," she admitted softly.

His head tilted to the side, and he studied her intently, violet eyes blazing. "Why me?"

"Because," was all she said.

"Glory."

Just tell him. She sighed. "Because I wanted you, and I knew I couldn't have you."

"You wanted me?" he asked huskily.

"You know I did." She watched him from the corner of her eye. He leaned back and stretched his legs out and up, the robe falling away and revealing his strong calves. There were calluses on the bottoms of his feet, as if he often ran through the forest without shoes on. Made her wonder if he wore any clothes at all. Her stomach quivered with the thought.

"Tell me about the first time you noticed me. Please."

Like she could deny him anything now. She thought back to that fateful day, and the quiver in her stomach became a needy ache. Well, another needy ache. She was consumed with them. He'd been moving boxes into this very house. She and her sisters had walked here to welcome him to town. When he spotted them, he'd frozen. Introductions had been made, and he'd smiled coolly but politely at Evie and Godiva. Glory, he'd simply nodded at before looking hastily away.

"I thought you were the most beautiful man I'd ever seen. The sun was shining over you lovingly, and you were sweating. Glistening. You'd taken off your shirt, and dirt smudged your chest."

His lips twitched. "I've noticed you have a thing for manly sweat."

"I do not."

"You placed me in a gladiator cell straight from battle, woman. You like men who do physical labor. Admit it."

"So what! There's nothing wrong with that."

"No, there isn't. It's cute." He didn't give her time to respond. "So why did you want to place me in chains tonight?"

She fought for breath. "You know why."

"Tell me. Say the words aloud."

"I—I'd decided to be with you. Just once. You know, to purge myself of you like you suggested before."

"And you thought you needed chains for that?"

"No. I just . . . I wanted to be in control of everything."

"I don't think so," he said with a shake of his head. "In the forest, you almost came when I pinned your wrists over your head and took control *away* from you. Right now, your nipples are hard, and your skin is besieged by goose bumps. You like where you are."

Her mouth dried as the realization settled inside her. He was right. She loved where she was. She loved that he could do anything he wanted with her, and she couldn't stop him. Didn't want to stop him.

Would one night be enough? She couldn't possibly learn all there was to know about his body, his pleasure . . . her own.

Oh, damn. Already she was doing what she'd sworn she wouldn't: falling deeper, wanting more. Fear dug sharp claws inside her. "Maybe this isn't a good idea," she said, squirming. "Maybe we should stop here and now and part. As friends. I won't hurt you again. You have my word. And you can even keep the pen."

"Oh, I'm keeping the pen," he said darkly, "but I'm not letting you go." He pushed to his feet. He was scowling.

"You're angry. Why? I'm setting you free from our war."

"I hate the thought of you walking out of this house—ever—and I don't understand it." The robe fell from his shoulders and onto the floor, pooling at his feet. She sucked in a breath and simply drank in his magnificence. He was harder than before, his erection so long it stretched higher than his navel.

He grabbed the pen and notebook and started writing. Before she could ask what he was doing, the chains fell away from her. Tentative, she eased up. But she didn't leave; she couldn't make herself, though common sense was screaming that she do so inside her mind. This was what she'd asked for.

"Thank you."

Fight for *me*. Wait. What? No.

"Not yet." He continued writing.

Quick as a snap, her weight returned, her bra and panty set nearly unraveling from the sudden excess. She gasped. Falon finally paused, his electric violet eyes all over her, eating her up.

Never taking his gaze from her, he locked the pen and paper inside a drawer on the nightstand, and then he was on the bed, crawling his way toward her.

· Eight ·

FALON had never wanted a woman the way he wanted Glory.

What was it about her that kept him coming back for more, despite her origins? Despite her actions and her words? She was exquisite, yes. Lush and soft, panting with arousal. She smelled of jasmine and magic, which was a feast to his senses. She was vulnerable yet courageous, daring and volatile. She had never and would never bow to him. She would fight him if he wronged her and always demand the very best from him.

He liked that. Liked who he was when he was with her. She made him be a better person. Honest and giving. Hopeful. And now that he thought about it, everything she'd done to him with that pen hadn't been malicious, it had been . . . foreplay.

His skin was nearly too tight for his bones as he stopped, his palms flattened beside Glory's knees. "Still want to leave?"

"No," she said breathlessly. She leaned back, propping her weight on her elbows. The plump mounds of her breasts strained beyond the bra.

"Want me?" He barely managed to work the words past the lump in his throat.

"Yes." No hesitation. "Maybe I'm crazy, but yes."

"Good, because I want you. All of you, this time." Fingers sliding under her knee, he lifted. His lips met the inside of her thigh, the cool stone of his necklace brushing against her, and she gasped.

He kissed again, his tongue stroking closer . . . closer . . .

Another gasp from her, followed by a shiver. "Hot," she said, trembling.

"Good?"

"Very."

"Hunter told me you write romance novels."

"Sometimes. Kiss again."

Grinning, he obeyed, running his tongue to the edge of her emerald panties.

"Oh, goodness." She fisted the sheets. He wanted those hands in his hair, holding on, holding forever.

She was perfect for this bed—his bed—he thought, staring down at her. A bright flame against black silk. "Have you ever thought of me when writing a love scene?"

"Yes." As though she'd read his mind, she gripped his head and pulled him down for another intimate kiss.

His cock throbbed at the thought, at the sight of her, at the taste of her, and he bit the inside of his cheek. Never had a woman appealed to so many of his senses. "What did you fantasize? What did I do to you?"

"Consumed every inch of me," she said, back arching, silently begging for more.

The best kind of answer.

Then she added, "We have one night together. I want everything I fantasized about."

One night. A muscle twitched underneath his eye. He didn't like the time limitation reminder but let it pass. For now. "Did it turn you on, what you wrote? Did you touch yourself?"

"Yes." Reaching up, she thrummed her nipples. "Like this."

"No. Between your legs. Show me."

She lifted her head, her eyes wide and focused on him. Her hands ceased moving on her breasts. "Wh-what?"

"Show me." Desperate for another taste of her, he kissed the center of her panties. They were wonderfully damp. He groaned, his mouth watered. "I want to see what *I've* been imagining."

"Oh." Slowly, so slowly, her hand slid down her stomach. "Like this?"

Licking around the seam of her panties, he fisted his cock. "More."

Slowly, so slowly, her hand circled the apex of her thighs, teasing. "Better?"

Down, he stroked. Up, squeezing tight. "Not yet."

He straightened; their gazes met again and held. "How about this?" Her fingers delved under the emerald lace. Her knees fell apart, and her lashes lowered. She cried out, hips undulating.

Shit. She *looked* like magic just then. Magic he craved. Down and up he continued to work himself, the sight of her so erotic he knew it was branded into his mind for eternity. *Touch her. Learn her.* He'd never wanted anything more.

"Stop," he commanded.

She stilled. Her eyes opened.

He released himself and latched onto her wrist, drawing her hand away from her body. She moaned, bit her bottom lip. "My turn." Leaning down, he lifted her fingers to his mouth and sucked one, then another inside. Her taste coated his tongue. "Like honey." And he needed more.

He laved his tongue inside her navel, gripping her panties and urging them from her legs. He thought she must have kicked them aside, because the bed bounced as he straightened.

"I've wanted to do this for a long time," he said, fingers

parting her wet folds. The thin patch of curls shielding her femininity were as bright a red as the hair on her head. Beautiful.

"Do it. *Please.*"

The desperation in her voice mirrored what he felt. He pressed her legs farther apart, spreading . . . spreading . . . so pretty. Pink and glistening. He lowered his head and stroked his tongue up the center.

"Falon," she cried.

He circled her clitoris as he sank a finger deep inside.

Her hands fisted in his hair just as he liked. "More."

Another finger joined the first, stretching her. All the while, he sucked and nipped at her. Had he ever tasted anyone so sweet? So addicting? Having her once wouldn't be enough, he realized. He'd need her over and over again. In every way imaginable. He just had to make *her* crave more.

As he licked her, he told her everything he wanted to do to her, how beautiful she was, how he needed her. Soon she was writhing, her head thrashing from side to side. He wanted to see her come. Had to see it, would die if he didn't. And then she was. Her inner walls clamped down on his tongue as she gasped and cried and even screamed.

He pulled from her, his gaze devouring her. Her eyes were closed, her teeth chewing on her bottom lip. Her skin was flushed. So quickly her chest rose and fell, lifting those rosy nipples like berries offered to a king.

A long while passed before she stilled. When she did, her eyelids cracked open.

He stayed just where he was, kneeling between her legs, cock rising proudly. "Like?"

"Like." She reached out and circled it with her fingers. "More."

A moan burst from his lips. "Glory."

"My turn," she said, squeezing him tighter. "I want to taste *you*."

He shook his head. "I don't want to come that way this first time, and if your mouth gets anywhere near my cock, I'll come."

She urged him forward, and he was helpless to do anything but follow wherever she led. "I'll stop before you come."

He found himself on his side. "No, you won't."

She grinned slowly, wickedly and rolled him to his back. Like a sea siren, she rose above him. "Okay, I won't. But you can try to force me to stop like the he-man you are."

Oh, the thought of her mouth on his shaft, hot and wet . . . her hair spilling over his thighs . . . His head fell back onto the pillow. "All right. But only because you insist."

She chuckled. "Such a martyr."

His cock twitched against her leg, her laughter as arousing as her touch.

Now she gasped. "Mmm, what was that for?"

"I like the sound of your laugh," he admitted. He wanted

to hear it. In the morning when he woke up, at lunch, at dinner. Just before bed.

"Sometimes you're as sweet as candy." She crawled down his body until her lips were poised over him. Just like he'd feared, his already intense sense of pleasure revved to a new level. "Probably taste like it, too."

He hoped so. He wanted her to like him, this.

"Tell me what you've fantasized about." Her warm breath stroked him, teased him.

He had to grip the sheets or he would soon be fisting her hair, and then there would be no stopping himself from coming in her mouth. "You. Doing this."

"What else?" She licked the tip, lapping up the glistening moisture already beaded there. "Mmm."

Shit. "Me, inside you."

Her teeth scraped the head, and he groaned at the delicious sensation. "What else?" she demanded. "Tell the truth, and you'll be rewarded. Isn't that how you like to work?"

"Pounding, hot, hard, wild, screaming, you bent over, me taking you from behind. My fingers on your clit, working it. You coming over and over."

As he spoke, she sucked him down, up, down. Taking him all the way to the back of her throat. He barely managed to get the words out, but he kept talking. Anything to continue that delicious pressure. One of her hands kneaded his balls, the other glided up his chest and flicked his nipple.

He felt attacked at every pleasure point, and he loved it.

He was bucking, unable to slow his movements, close to the edge. If she kept this up, he really would—*Shit, shit, shit.* Falon grabbed her shoulders and jerked her up. Her lips were swollen and wet, she was panting, her desire clearly renewed.

She moaned in disappointment. "I wasn't done."

"Condom," he said, the word more a snarl. "Now."

Her pupils were dilated, her cheeks flushed as she gazed around wildly. "Where are they?"

Damn, where had he placed them? He searched, saw two silver packets resting on the floor. He'd thought ahead, for once. He reached out, way out, grabbed one and ripped it open with his teeth. Motions jerky, he straightened and worked it over his length.

His hands settled on Glory's thighs and spread them as wide as they would go. Her wet, needy core was poised over his cock, just like her mouth had been. "Ride me."

"I thought—you said behind."

"Next time," he said, and then she was pressing, he was arching, and he was all the way inside her, surging deep, taking all of her that he could get.

Her head fell back, her hair tickling his legs. Her breasts arched forward, and he cupped the small of her back, jerking her forward. When those hardened buds abraded his chest, he growled out, "Yeah, this is what I needed."

"Feels so good."

"Kiss."

"Please."

He pounded in and out of her as their lips met. His tongue thrust inside, and she eagerly welcomed it, rolling it with her own. Their teeth clashed together once, twice, but that didn't douse the intensity.

Every other woman he'd ever been with faded to the back of his mind as if they'd never existed. There was only Glory. There was only here and now. Eternity—with her.

"Falon," she gasped, and he knew she was close.

He reached between them and thrummed her clitoris. That was all she'd needed. She came in a rush, squeezing at his cock, crying his name again and again, nails raking his chest.

He, too, fell over the edge. And when he came, it was the strongest of his life. Every muscle he possessed locked and released, spasming. Blood rushed through his veins, so hot it blistered everything it touched.

"Glory," he chanted, and it was a prayer for more. More of her, more of this.

NOW *I've gone and done it*, Glory thought. She was snuggled into Falon's side, warm and sated—more so than she'd ever been before. He was asleep, his breathing smooth. Even in slumber, his hand traced up and down her spine as though he couldn't stop touching her.

I love him.

There, she'd admitted it. She did. She loved him. Would

have liked to spend forever with him. Making love, talking, laughing. Impossible.

She was a witch, and there was nothing she could do about that. She possessed magic powers. That wasn't something she could switch off. Not for long, anyway. And Falon would always fear her because of it, no matter what he claimed.

All these months, she'd gagged every time she'd seen her sisters with their boyfriends. Her chest had ached, and she'd assumed the ache was from disgust not love. Now she was experiencing the emotion for herself. The ache for what could not be.

Her eyes filled with tears. She loved Falon, but she couldn't have him. Even though he thought he wanted more from her. He'd said as much before falling asleep. She hadn't answered, hadn't known what to say. But she could just imagine him cringing during their first fight, suspecting her of evildoing. She could just imagine the accusations he'd hurl at her every time something went wrong in his life.

That would destroy her. Better to walk away now, as planned. It was the only way her heart could survive.

Gingerly, Glory slipped from his body, from the bed. Her legs were so shaky she almost fell. Since she'd written herself here without any real clothes, she borrowed a pair of sweats and a T-shirt from Falon.

Before she put them on, she held them to her nose and inhaled deeply. They smelled of him, like soap, dark spices, and strength. A tear fell. Once dressed, she walked to the edge of the bed. Still he slept soundly. Must not have gotten any rest these past few days. He'd probably feared she'd attack with her pen at any moment.

What if things could be different? What if there was a chance they could make it work?

He looked so peaceful. His dark hair was in disarray against the pillow. His face was flushed with lingering pleasure. The sheet had fallen, revealing the entire expanse of his mouthwatering chest.

Who are you trying to fool? Make it work? Please. Those silly tears began falling in earnest. She was going to miss him. Taunting him, being with him, sparring with him, had been fun. He was witty, and he was warm. He was wild and protective and a lover who cared more about her pleasure than his own.

His fingers flexed over the part of the mattress she'd occupied.

Her heart stopped beating. One step, two, she backed away from the bed. Any moment, he would probably wake up. What would he say to her? What would he do?

Doesn't matter.

Glory pivoted on her heel and stalked quietly from his house. They only lived a mile apart, and she'd traveled the forest many times before, so she entered the night without hesitation.

She left her heart with Falon.

Nine

WHEN Falon woke up alone, he was not happy.

When he rushed to Glory's house and discovered she had packed a bag and taken off, telling no one where she planned to stay, he was angry.

When he drove around town, asking if anyone had seen her and found that no one had, he was beyond furious!

Why had she left him?

To punish him? He didn't think so. They were past that point now, he knew it, and she wasn't the type to do so without gloating—something he loved about her. Loved. Yes. He loved her. She was his woman, the other piece of him. He knew that now, and so there would be no more denying it. The fact that she was a witch didn't matter anymore. He'd rather have her and her powers than be without her.

Had she left because she was . . . scared?

Yes, he thought. *Yes.* Well, he was scared, too. New relationships were always scary, but this one more so than most. They'd been at odds for a while. But they'd also just had the best sex of his life. Addictive sex. He'd just have to prove they could be together, that he wouldn't hurt her, wouldn't stop loving her. But how?

You still have the pen.

The thought slammed into him with the force of a jackhammer, and he grinned. He rushed back home.

GLORY was inside her Ford Taurus one moment and back home the next. Brow puckered in confusion, she gazed around. "What the hell?"

Her sisters were sitting in the living room, reading *Witch Weekly*. They glanced up at the sound of her voice.

"Oh, there you are," Godiva said.

"Where have you been?" Evie asked. "Falon's been desperate to find you."

She gulped. Rubbed her stomach. Falon. The pen. Damn it! He was using the pen. Why, why, why? She'd almost made a clean getaway. Had almost given them a clean break. Clean. Yeah, right.

A knock sounded at the door.

She whipped around, eyes wide. Was it Falon?

Another knock, this one harder.

"Well, aren't you going to answer it?" Godiva asked.

"Open up, Glory. I know you're in there. I made sure of it."

Falon's deep, dark voice filled her head, and she almost fainted. He'd truly come here. Why? He could have written her anywhere, but he'd written her inside her own home and knocked on her door.

"Glory!" Evie laughed. "Don't just stand there."

If he was going to ask—again—for more from her than one night, she wouldn't be able to turn him down. She'd sobbed like a baby the entire drive away from town. In fact, her face was probably swollen and red even now. Where she'd been headed, she hadn't known. She'd just needed to put distance between them, or she would have forgotten all the reasons to stay away and gone to him.

"Please," he said, and he sounded tortured. She could very easily imagine his hands resting on the door, his forehead pressing into the wood.

Shaky legs walked her to the entrance. Her palm was sweating so she had trouble twisting the knob. What was she going to find? Slowly, she pulled open the only thing blocking the man she loved from her view.

Falon stood there, wearing a trench coat and nothing else. Not even shoes. She blinked in surprise. *So* not what she had expected.

"What are you doing here?" she managed to get out.

Her sisters crowded behind her.

"Looking good, Falon," Evie said.

"Nice," Godiva said.

His cheeks bloomed bright red, but his attention remained focused on Glory. "I want you in my life."

Her stomach twisted painfully. "That wouldn't be smart. We'd fight, you'd hate me, fear my powers."

As she spoke, he was shaking his head. "You're different from the other witches I knew, I know that deep down. Even though you had every right to be angry with me, you were never malicious."

"You think so now, but what about tomorrow? Or the next day?"

Again he shook his head. "Not gonna happen."

"You can't guarantee that."

"But I *can* guarantee that I love you."

Her eyes nearly bugged out, his words echoing inside her brain. "Wh-what?"

"I love you."

Godiva gasped. "Did you hear that, Evie?"

"I'm standing right here. Of course I heard. Glory, what do you have to say to him?"

"Give me a chance," he begged. "I don't deserve it, I know I don't, but I'll do anything to get it. I need you in my life."

She covered her mouth with a shaky hand. This was too much, too good to believe.

He forged ahead. "You once came to my door, wanting a night with me. Now I've come to your door, wanting an